THE MYSTICAL PENCIL

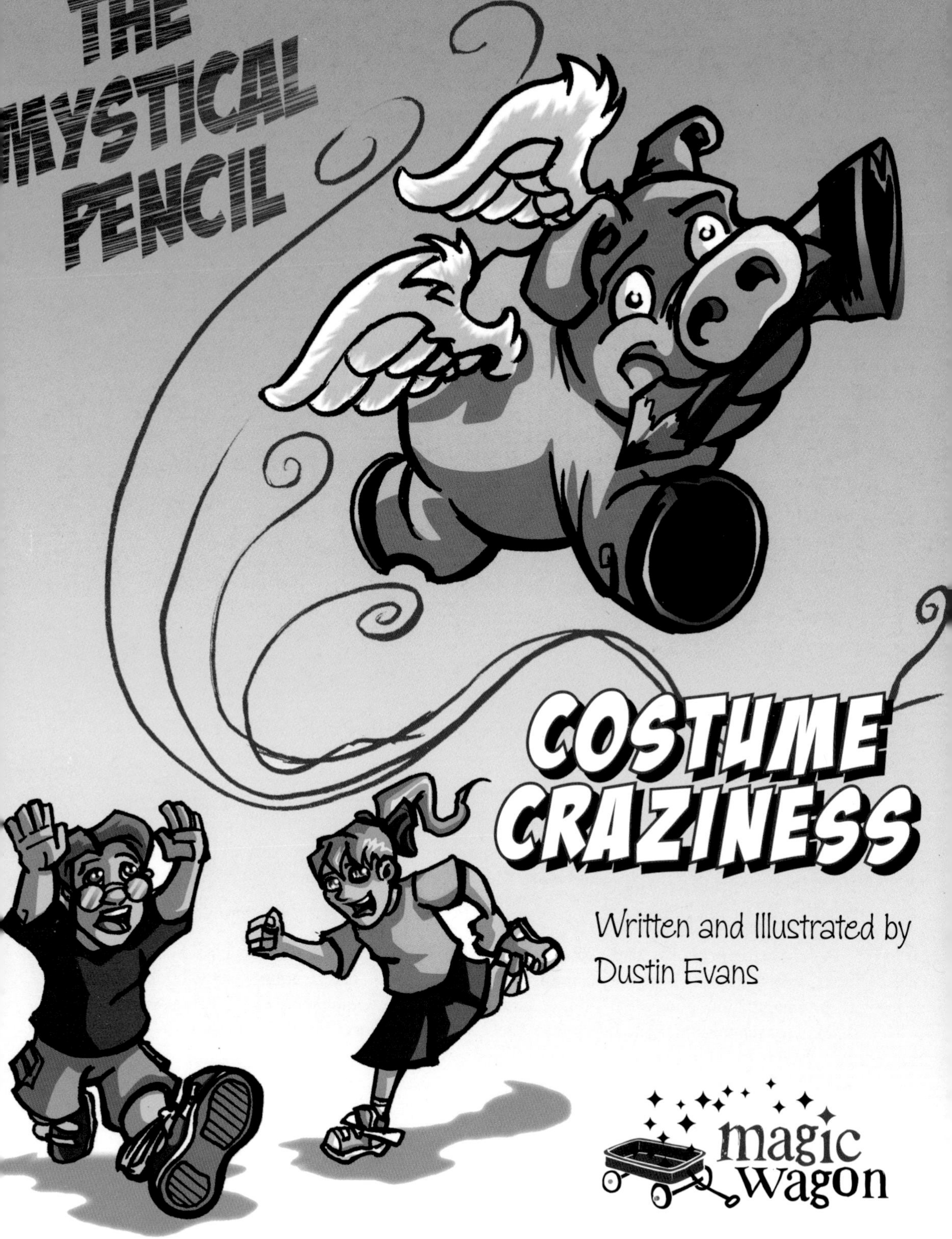

COSTUME CRAZINESS

Written and Illustrated by
Dustin Evans

magic wagon

visit us at
www.abdopublishing.com

Published by Magic Wagon, a division of the ABDO Group, PO Box 398166, Minneapolis, MN 55439. Copyright © 2013 by Abdo Consulting Group, Inc. International copyrights reserved in all countries. All rights reserved. No part of this book may be reproduced in any form without written permission from the publisher.

Graphic Planet™ is a trademark and logo of Magic Wagon.

Printed in the United States of America, North Mankato, Minnesota.
102012
012013
This book contains at least 10% recycled materials.

Written and Illustrated by Dustin Evans
Edited by Stephanie Hedlund and Rochelle Baltzer
Cover art by Dustin Evans
Cover design by Neil Klinepier

Library of Congress Cataloging-in-Publication Data

Evans, Dustin, 1982-
  Costume craziness / written & illustrated by Dustin Evans.
    p. cm. -- (The mystical pencil)
  Summary: Sara finds the mystical pencil on the sidewalk where Alex dropped it and brings it to school on costume design day--and before Alex can explain the danger the school is full of flying pigs and barnyard animals.
  ISBN 978-1-61641-926-4
1. Pencils--Comic books, strips, etc. 2. Pencils--Juvenile fiction. 3. Elementary schools--Comic books, strips, etc. 4. Elementary schools--Juvenile fiction. 5. Imagination--Comic books, strips, etc. 6. Imagination--Juvenile fiction. 7. Graphic novels. [1. Graphic novels. 2. Pencils--Fiction. 3. Elementary schools--Fiction. 4. Schools--Fiction. 5. Imagination--Fiction.] I. Title.
  PZ7.7.E92Cos 2013
  741.5'973--dc23
                         2012027926

Contents

Previously in *A Medieval Mess . . .*

Alex's dad returned from an archaeological dig and brought back many artifacts. When Alex needed a pencil to finish his project on the Renaissance time period, he got an old, beat-up one from his dad's bag.

That beat-up pencil didn't look like much, but it had great powers! The monster Alex drew suddenly came to life! Alex continued to draw with the Mystical Pencil, trying to set things right. But it only got worse.

Soon, there was a knight, a king, a queen, peasants, a sculptor, and more! When the new characters started hunting the monster, Alex had to think quickly to make things right.

Alex drew the morning as if it were all a dream. He woke up to find everything was back to normal... but one thing was missing —the Mystical Pencil! Its adventure continues now...

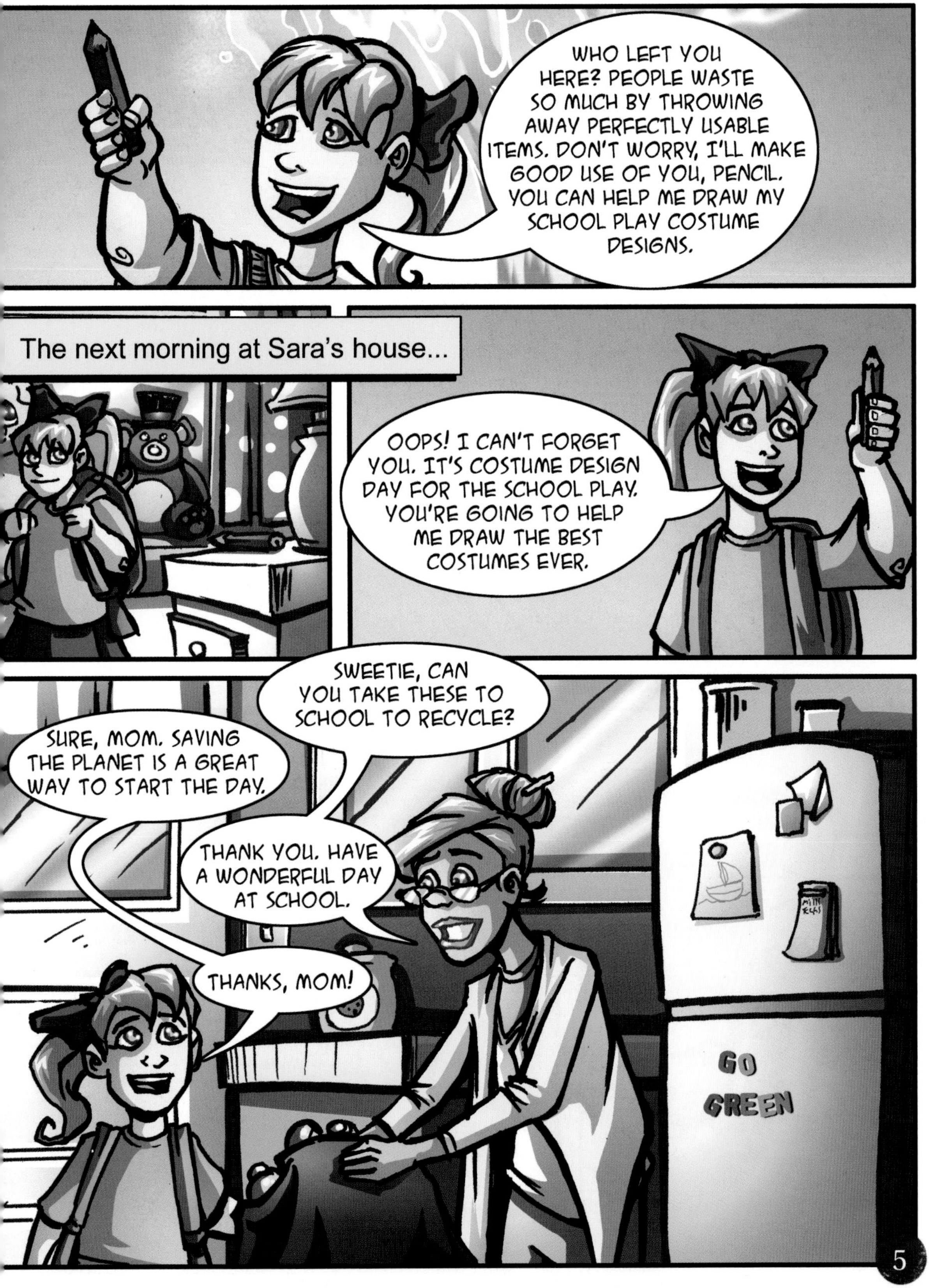

WHO LEFT YOU HERE? PEOPLE WASTE SO MUCH BY THROWING AWAY PERFECTLY USABLE ITEMS. DON'T WORRY, I'LL MAKE GOOD USE OF YOU, PENCIL. YOU CAN HELP ME DRAW MY SCHOOL PLAY COSTUME DESIGNS.
The next morning at Sara's house...
OOPS! I CAN'T FORGET YOU. IT'S COSTUME DESIGN DAY FOR THE SCHOOL PLAY. YOU'RE GOING TO HELP ME DRAW THE BEST COSTUMES EVER.
SWEETIE, CAN YOU TAKE THESE TO SCHOOL TO RECYCLE?
SURE, MOM. SAVING THE PLANET IS A GREAT WAY TO START THE DAY.
THANK YOU. HAVE A WONDERFUL DAY AT SCHOOL.
THANKS, MOM!
GO GREEN

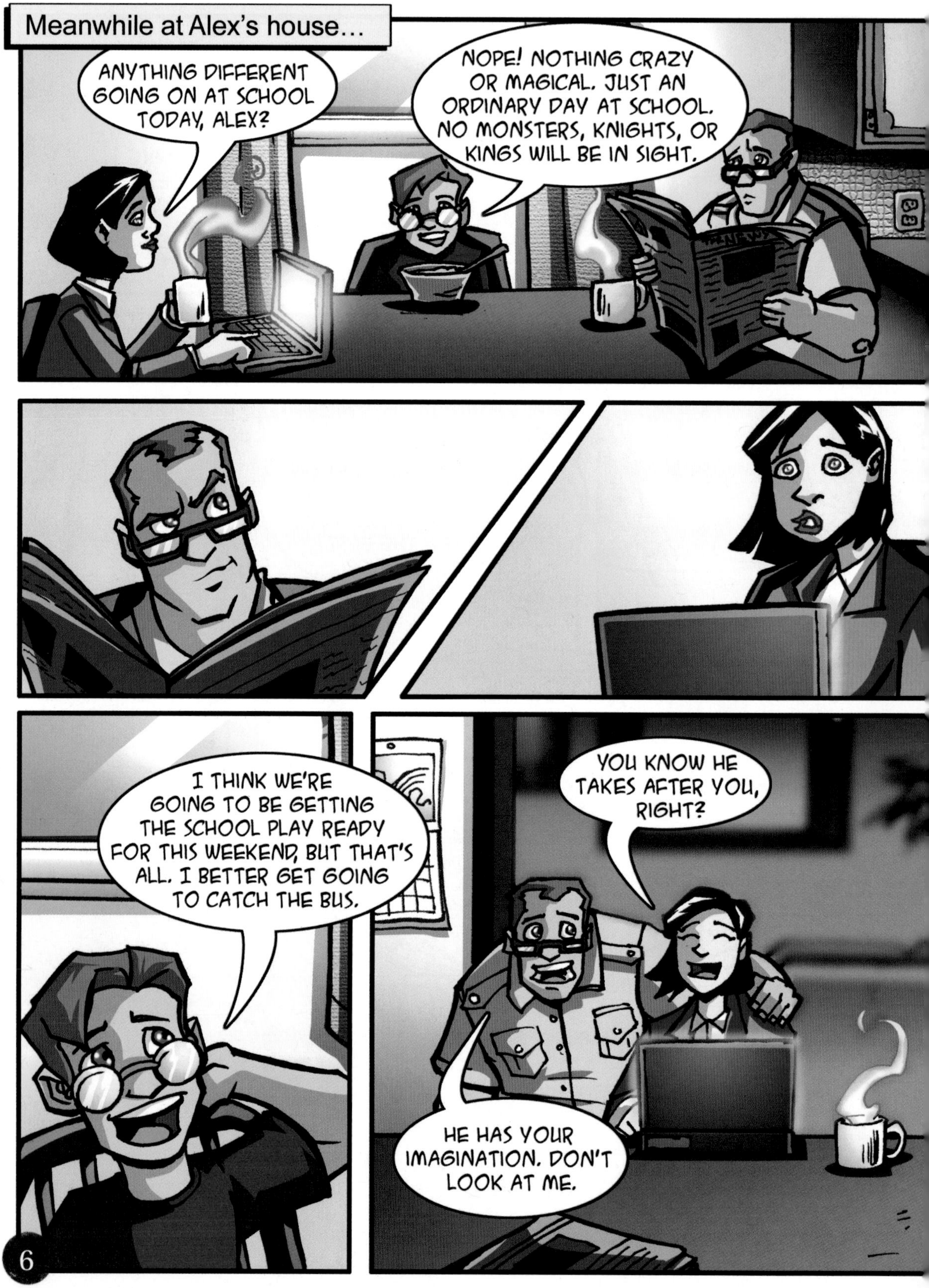
Meanwhile at Alex's house...
ANYTHING DIFFERENT GOING ON AT SCHOOL TODAY, ALEX?
NOPE! NOTHING CRAZY OR MAGICAL. JUST AN ORDINARY DAY AT SCHOOL. NO MONSTERS, KNIGHTS, OR KINGS WILL BE IN SIGHT.
I THINK WE'RE GOING TO BE GETTING THE SCHOOL PLAY READY FOR THIS WEEKEND, BUT THAT'S ALL. I BETTER GET GOING TO CATCH THE BUS.
YOU KNOW HE TAKES AFTER YOU, RIGHT?
HE HAS YOUR IMAGINATION. DON'T LOOK AT ME.

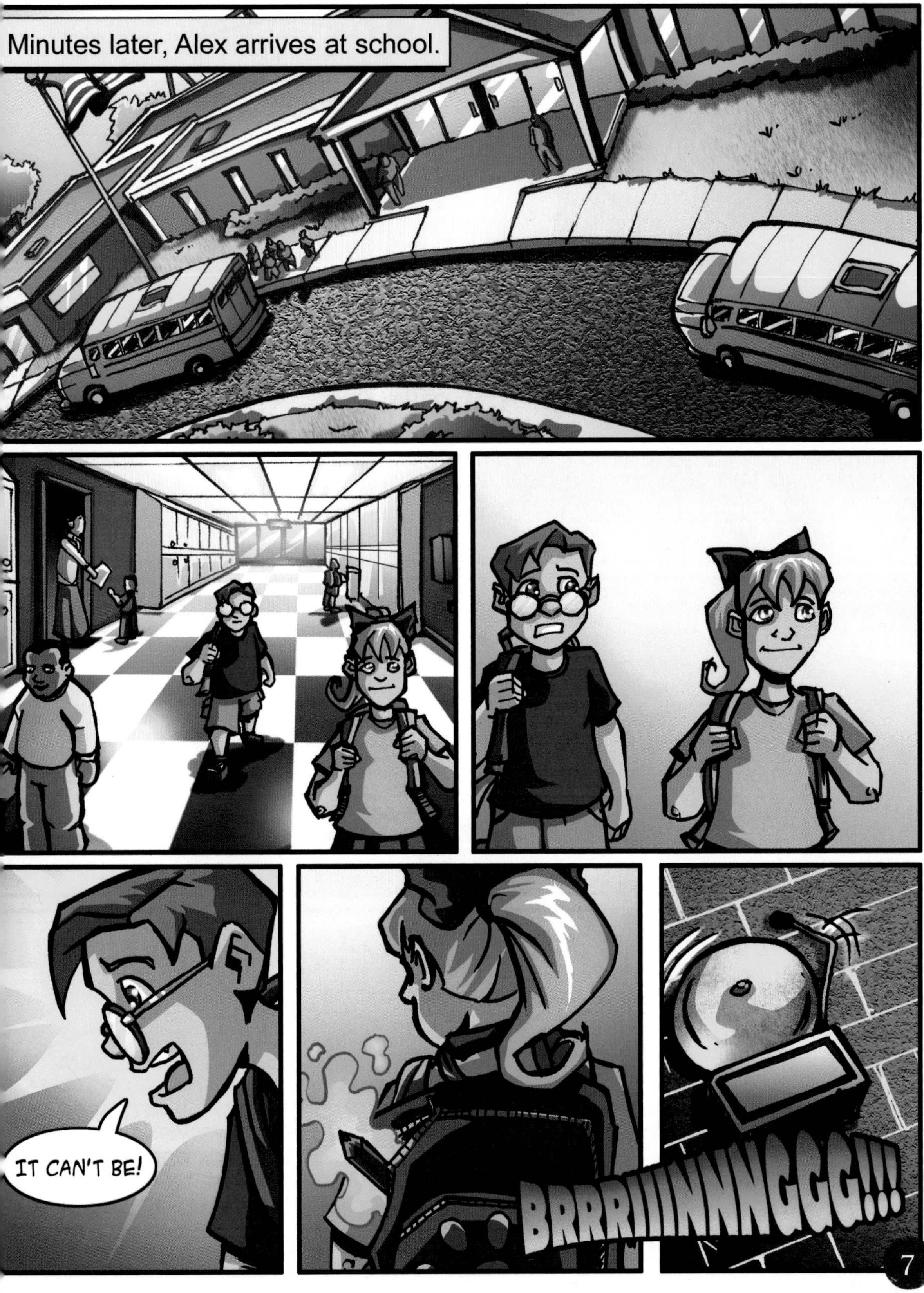
Minutes later, Alex arrives at school.
IT CAN'T BE!
BRRRIIIINNNNGGG!!!

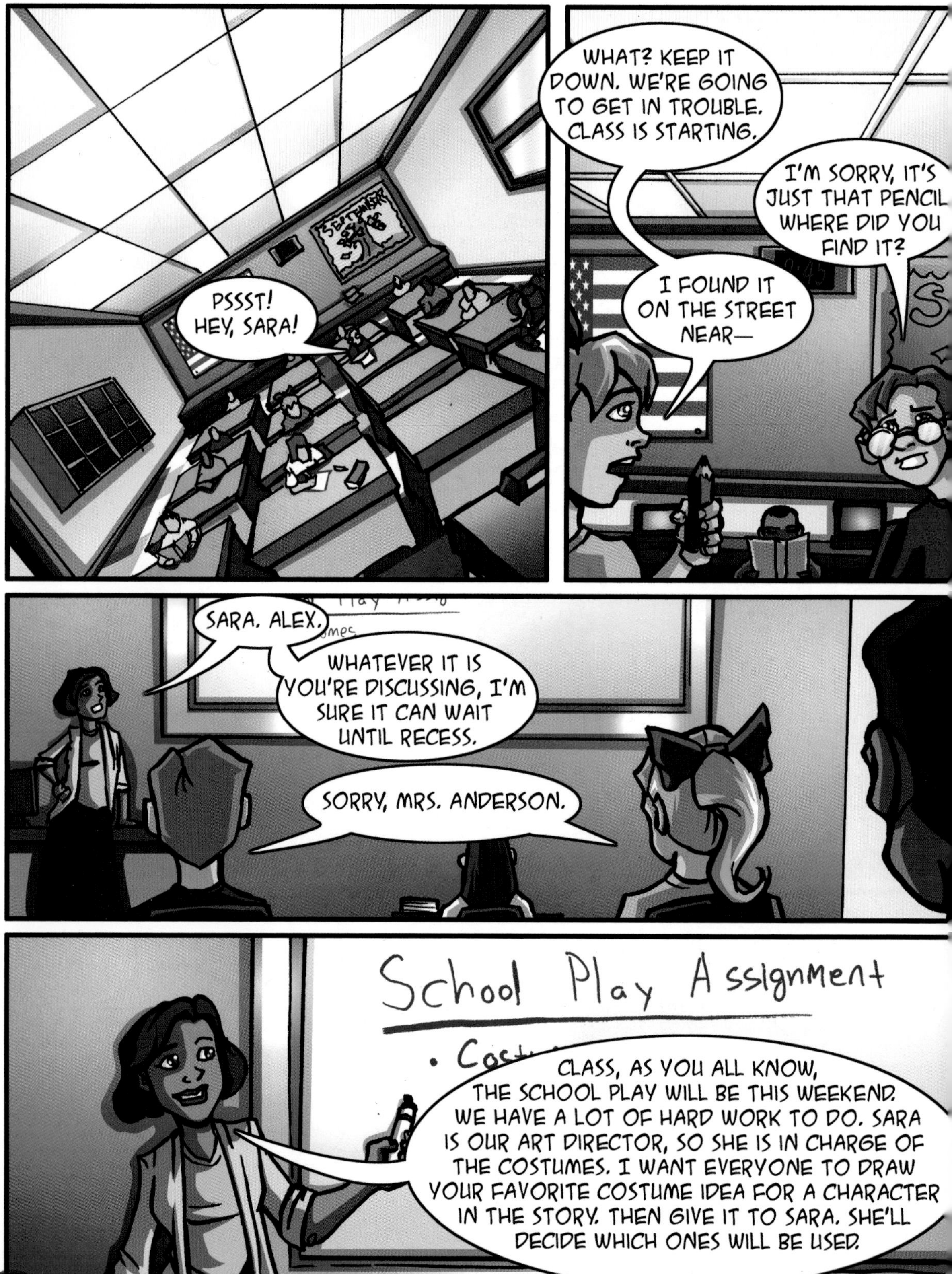
PSSST! HEY, SARA!
WHAT? KEEP IT DOWN. WE'RE GOING TO GET IN TROUBLE. CLASS IS STARTING.
I'M SORRY, IT'S JUST THAT PENCIL WHERE DID YOU FIND IT?
I FOUND IT ON THE STREET NEAR—
SARA. ALEX.
WHATEVER IT IS YOU'RE DISCUSSING, I'M SURE IT CAN WAIT UNTIL RECESS.
SORRY, MRS. ANDERSON.
School Play Assignment
CLASS, AS YOU ALL KNOW, THE SCHOOL PLAY WILL BE THIS WEEKEND. WE HAVE A LOT OF HARD WORK TO DO. SARA IS OUR ART DIRECTOR, SO SHE IS IN CHARGE OF THE COSTUMES. I WANT EVERYONE TO DRAW YOUR FAVORITE COSTUME IDEA FOR A CHARACTER IN THE STORY. THEN GIVE IT TO SARA. SHE'LL DECIDE WHICH ONES WILL BE USED.

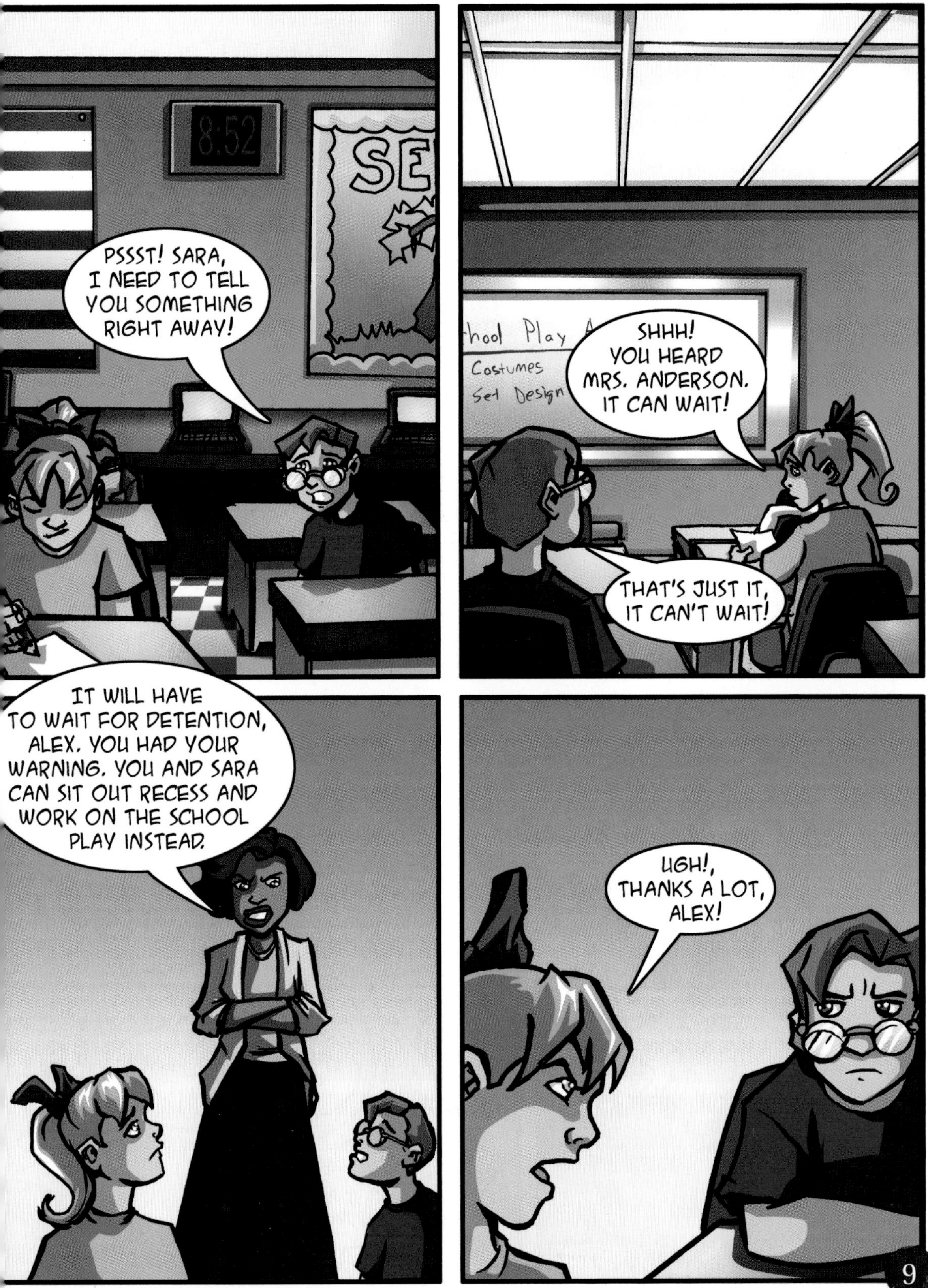
8:52
SE
PSSST! SARA, I NEED TO TELL YOU SOMETHING RIGHT AWAY!
School Play A
Costumes
Set Design
SHHH! YOU HEARD MRS. ANDERSON. IT CAN WAIT!
THAT'S JUST IT, IT CAN'T WAIT!
IT WILL HAVE TO WAIT FOR DETENTION, ALEX. YOU HAD YOUR WARNING. YOU AND SARA CAN SIT OUT RECESS AND WORK ON THE SCHOOL PLAY INSTEAD.
UGH!, THANKS A LOT, ALEX!

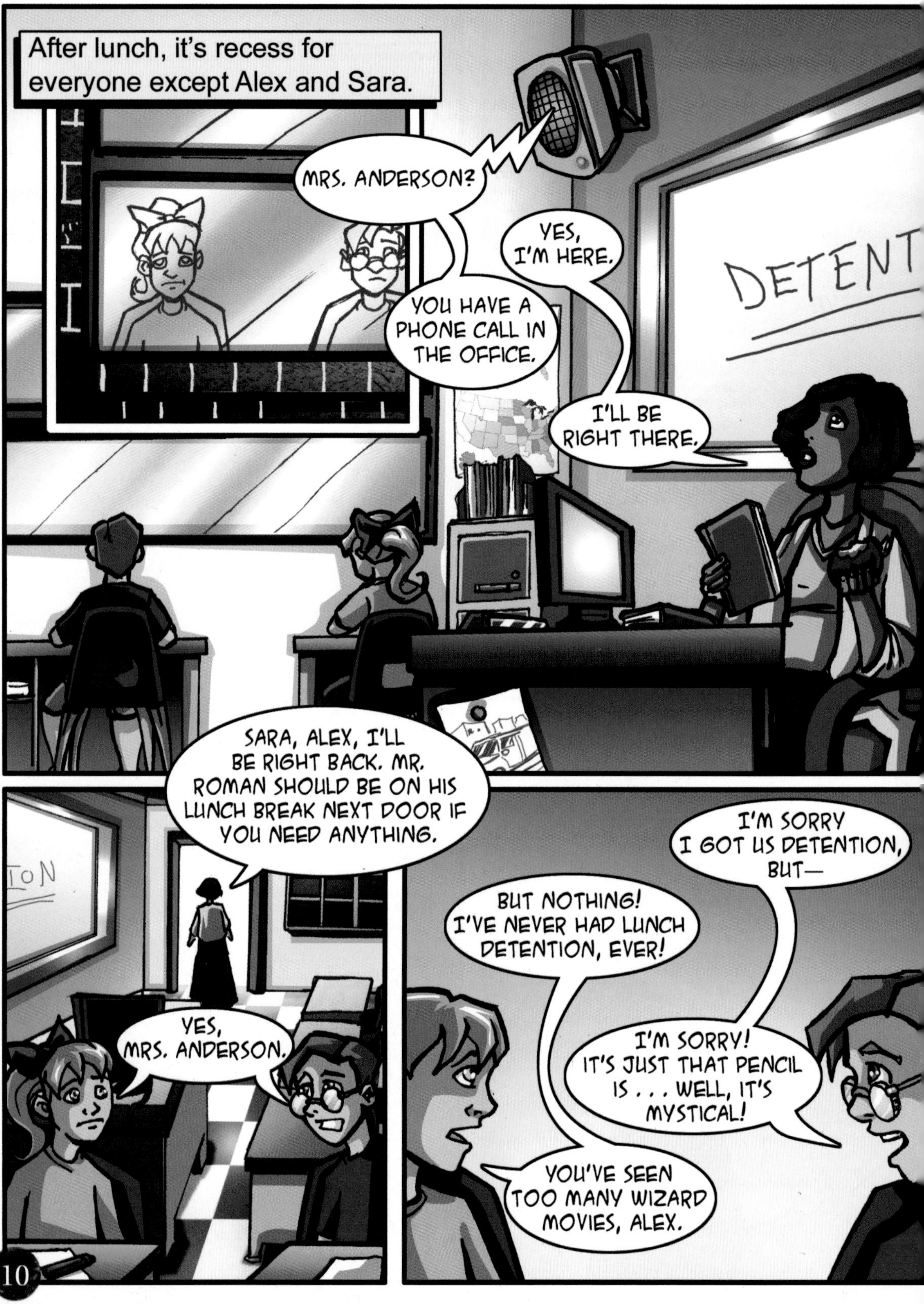
After lunch, it's recess for everyone except Alex and Sara.
MRS. ANDERSON?
YES, I'M HERE.
YOU HAVE A PHONE CALL IN THE OFFICE.
I'LL BE RIGHT THERE.
DETENT
SARA, ALEX, I'LL BE RIGHT BACK. MR. ROMAN SHOULD BE ON HIS LUNCH BREAK NEXT DOOR IF YOU NEED ANYTHING.
TION
YES, MRS. ANDERSON.
I'M SORRY I GOT US DETENTION, BUT—
BUT NOTHING! I'VE NEVER HAD LUNCH DETENTION, EVER!
I'M SORRY! IT'S JUST THAT PENCIL IS . . . WELL, IT'S MYSTICAL!
YOU'VE SEEN TOO MANY WIZARD MOVIES, ALEX.

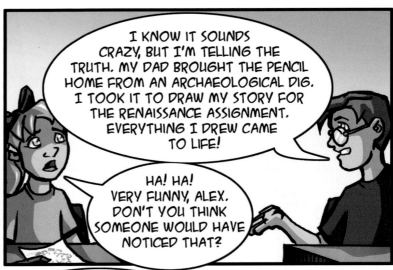

I KNOW IT SOUNDS CRAZY, BUT I'M TELLING THE TRUTH. MY DAD BROUGHT THE PENCIL HOME FROM AN ARCHAEOLOGICAL DIG. I TOOK IT TO DRAW MY STORY FOR THE RENAISSANCE ASSIGNMENT. EVERYTHING I DREW CAME TO LIFE!

HA! HA! VERY FUNNY, ALEX. DON'T YOU THINK SOMEONE WOULD HAVE NOTICED THAT?

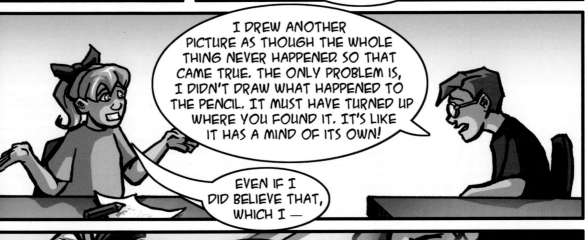

I DREW ANOTHER PICTURE AS THOUGH THE WHOLE THING NEVER HAPPENED. SO THAT CAME TRUE. THE ONLY PROBLEM IS, I DIDN'T DRAW WHAT HAPPENED TO THE PENCIL. IT MUST HAVE TURNED UP WHERE YOU FOUND IT. IT'S LIKE IT HAS A MIND OF ITS OWN!

EVEN IF I DID BELIEVE THAT, WHICH I —

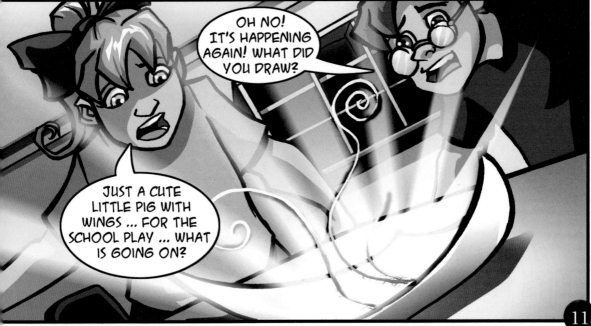

OH NO! IT'S HAPPENING AGAIN! WHAT DID YOU DRAW?

JUST A CUTE LITTLE PIG WITH WINGS ... FOR THE SCHOOL PLAY ... WHAT IS GOING ON?

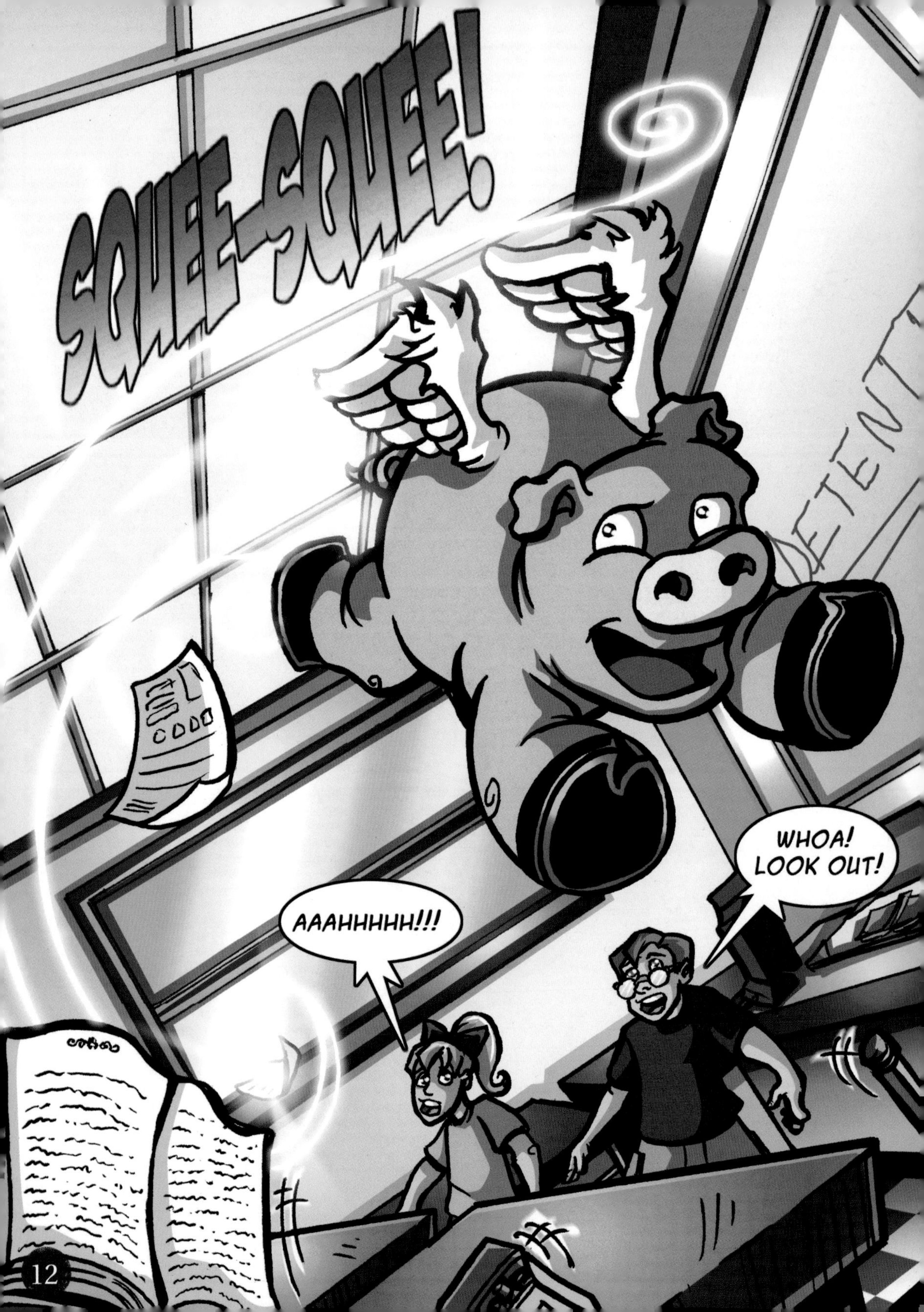
SQUEE-SQUEE!
WHOA! LOOK OUT!
AAAHHHHH!!!

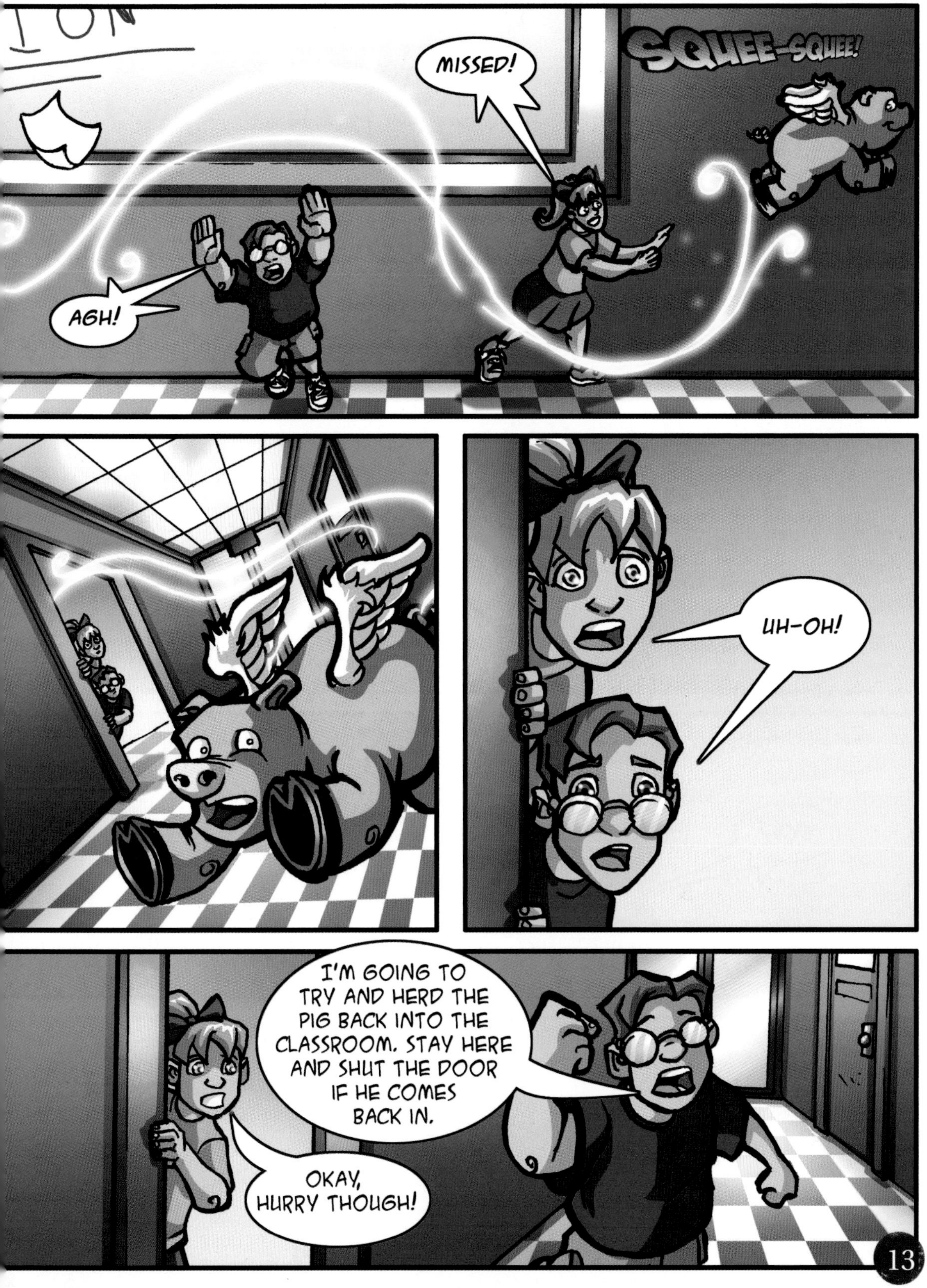

MISSED!
SQUEE-SQUEE!
AGH!
UH-OH!
I'M GOING TO TRY AND HERD THE PIG BACK INTO THE CLASSROOM. STAY HERE AND SHUT THE DOOR IF HE COMES BACK IN.
OKAY, HURRY THOUGH!

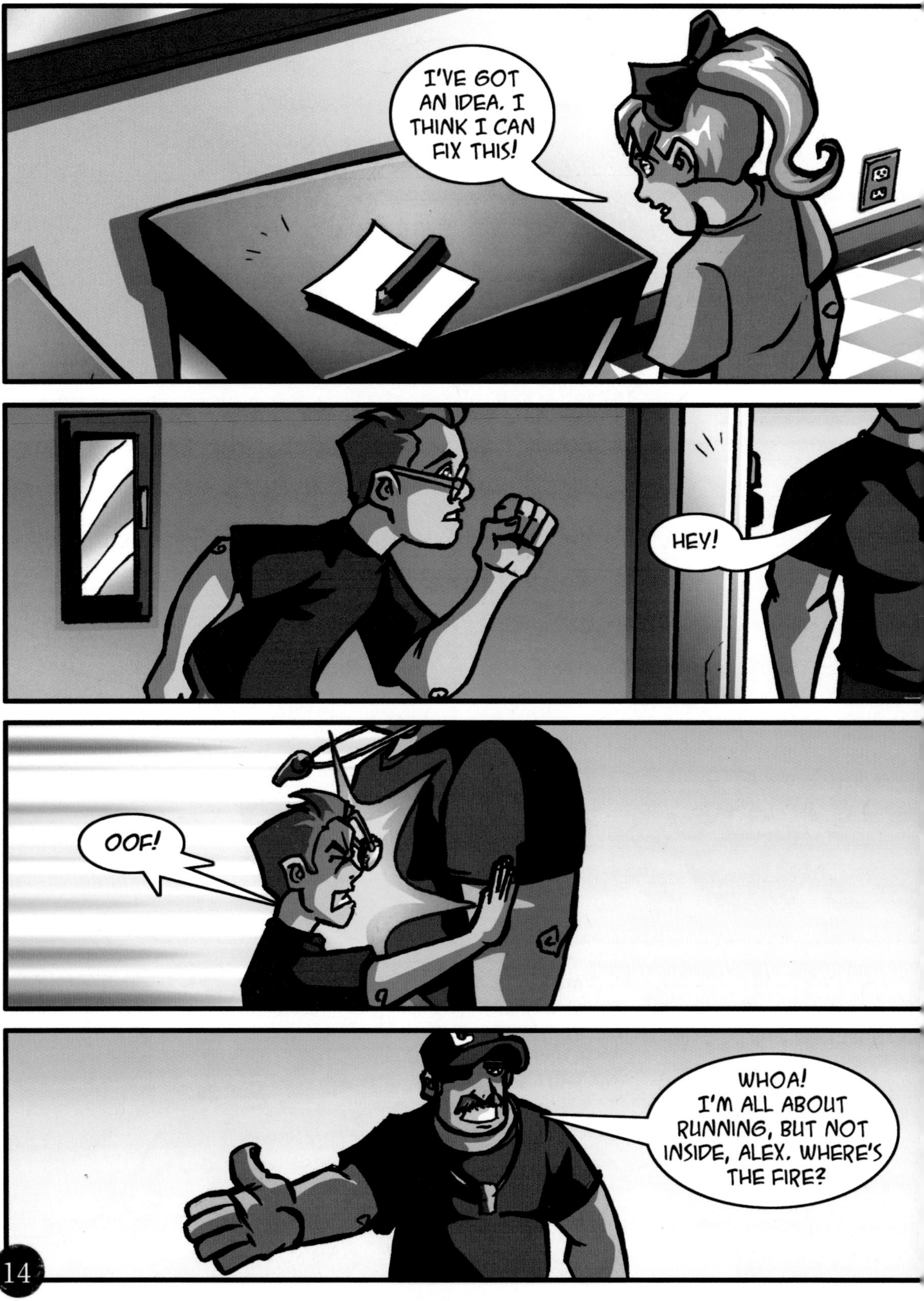
I'VE GOT AN IDEA. I THINK I CAN FIX THIS!
HEY!
OOF!
WHOA! I'M ALL ABOUT RUNNING, BUT NOT INSIDE, ALEX. WHERE'S THE FIRE?

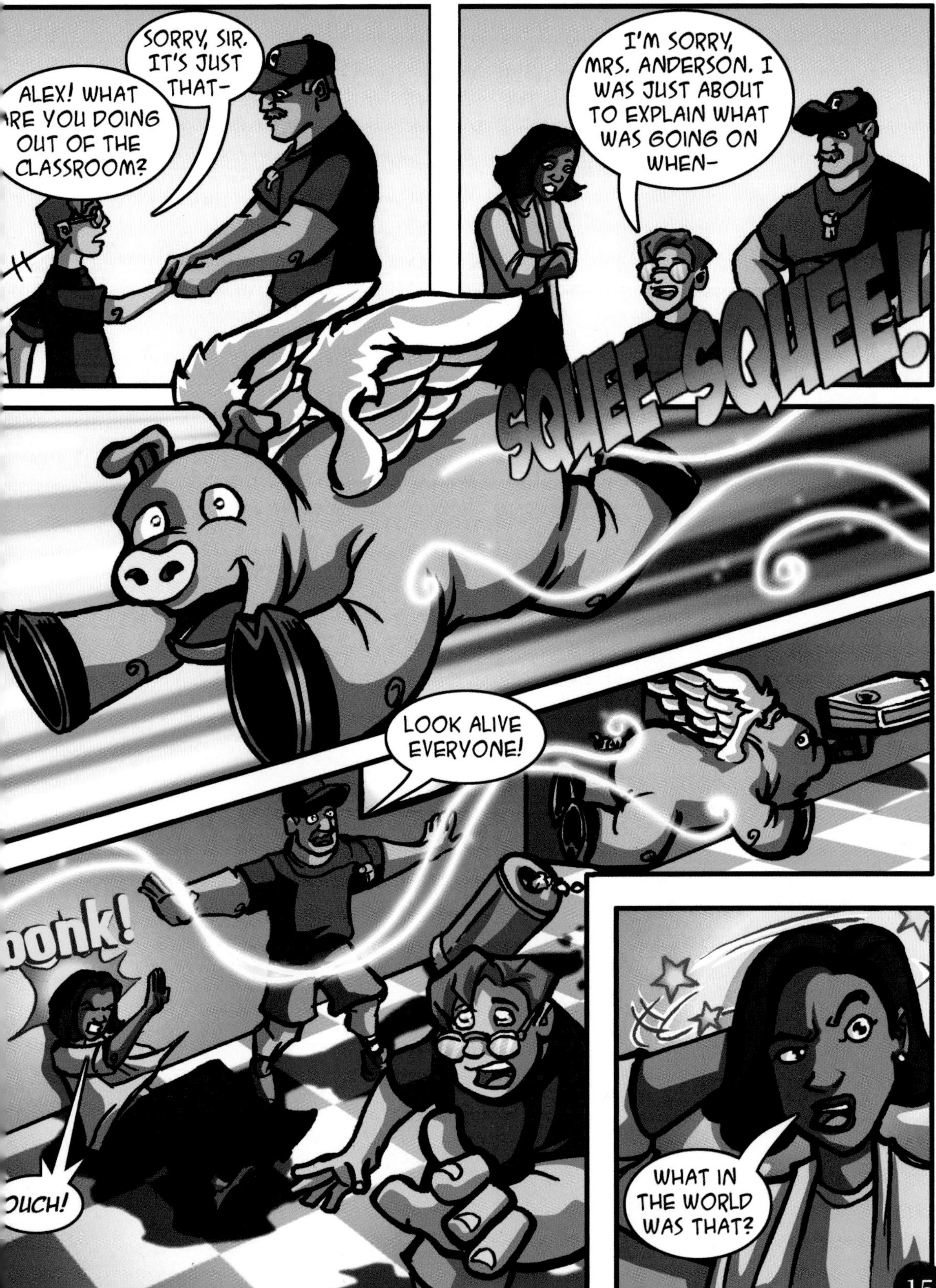
ALEX! WHAT ARE YOU DOING OUT OF THE CLASSROOM?
SORRY, SIR. IT'S JUST THAT-
I'M SORRY, MRS. ANDERSON. I WAS JUST ABOUT TO EXPLAIN WHAT WAS GOING ON WHEN-
SQUEE-SQUEE!
LOOK ALIVE EVERYONE!
bonk!
OUCH!
WHAT IN THE WORLD WAS THAT?

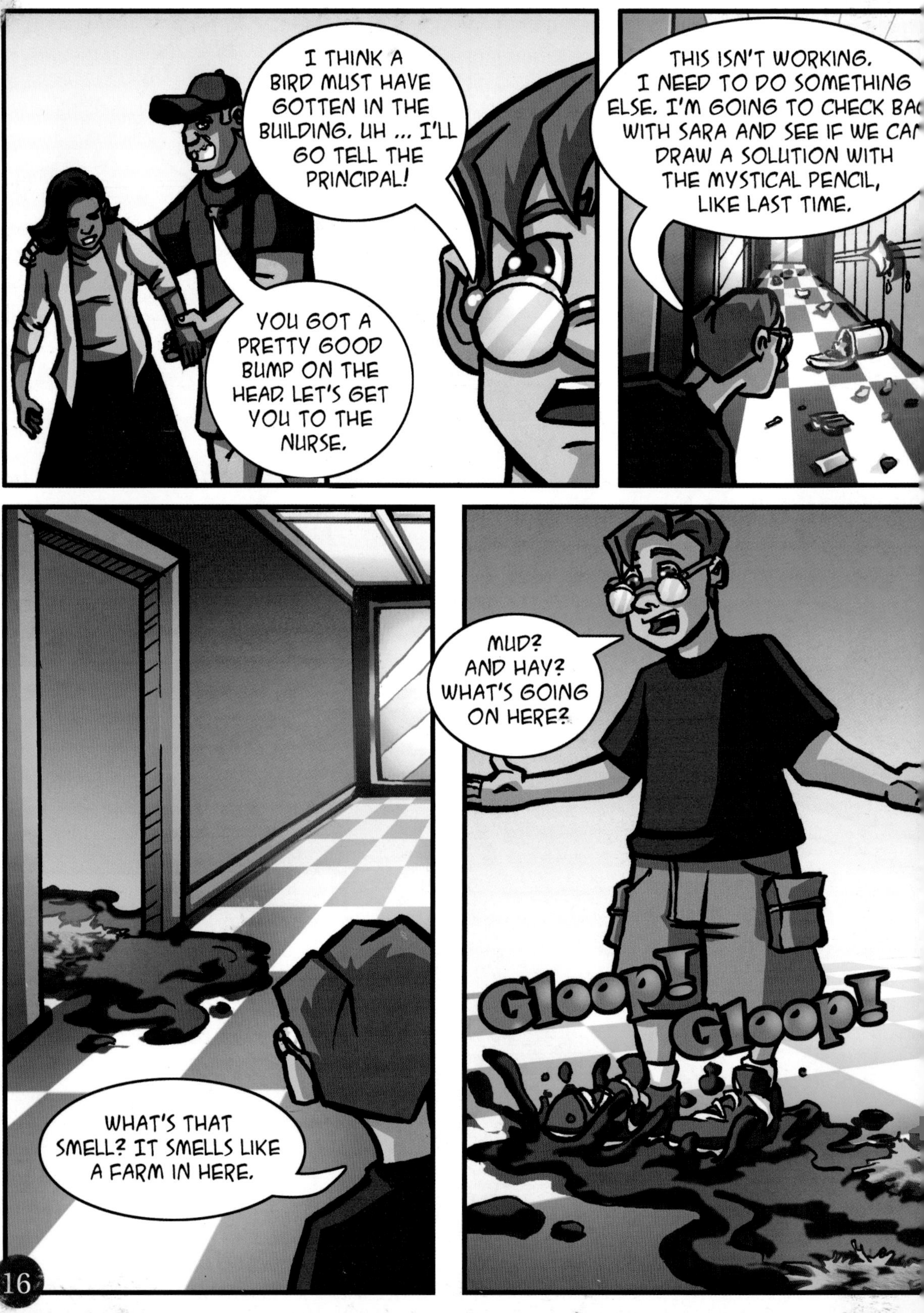
I THINK A BIRD MUST HAVE GOTTEN IN THE BUILDING. UH ... I'LL GO TELL THE PRINCIPAL!
YOU GOT A PRETTY GOOD BUMP ON THE HEAD. LET'S GET YOU TO THE NURSE.
THIS ISN'T WORKING. I NEED TO DO SOMETHING ELSE. I'M GOING TO CHECK BAC WITH SARA AND SEE IF WE CAN DRAW A SOLUTION WITH THE MYSTICAL PENCIL, LIKE LAST TIME.
WHAT'S THAT SMELL? IT SMELLS LIKE A FARM IN HERE.
MUD? AND HAY? WHAT'S GOING ON HERE?
Gloop! Gloop!

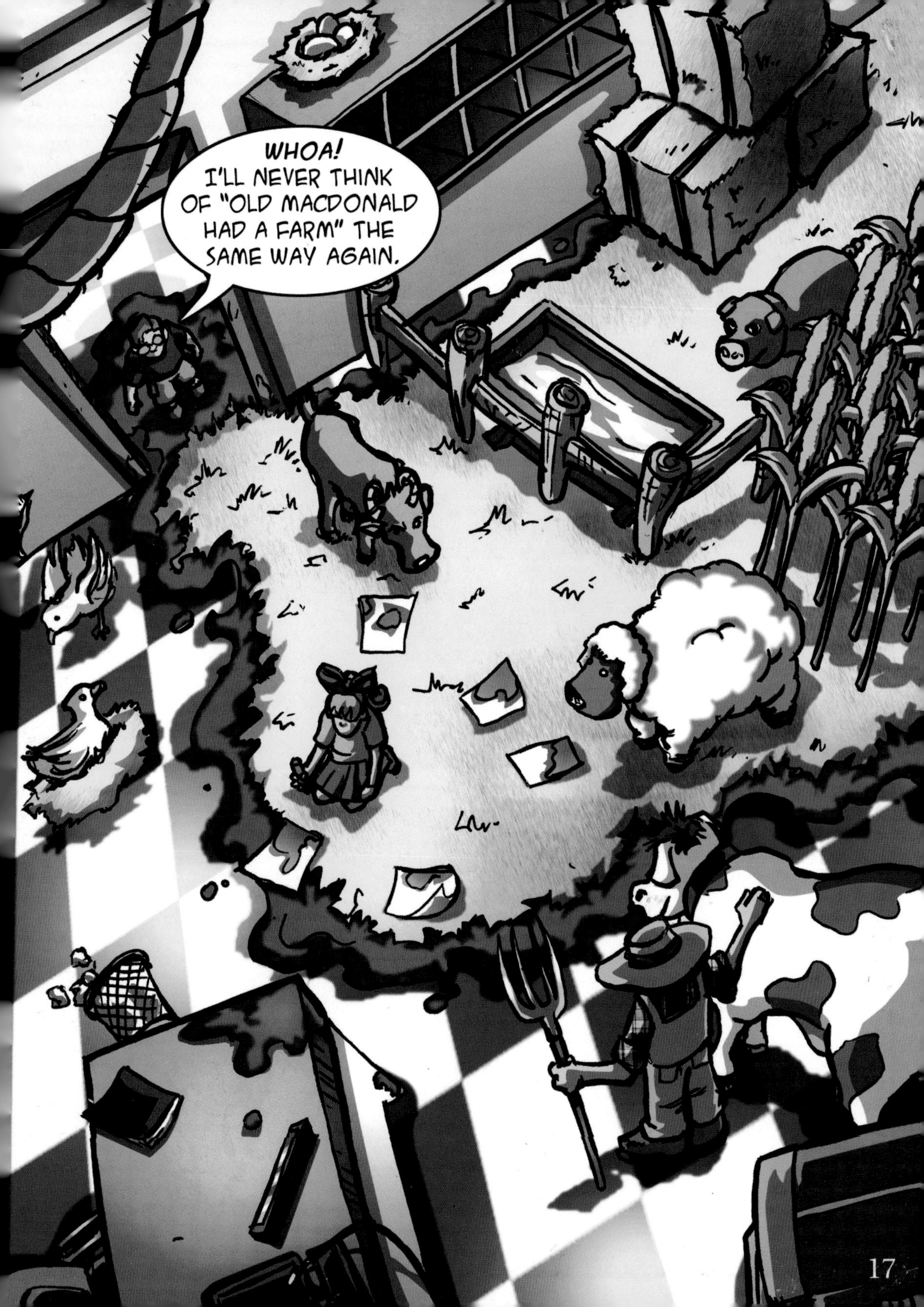
WHOA!
I'LL NEVER THINK OF "OLD MACDONALD HAD A FARM" THE SAME WAY AGAIN.

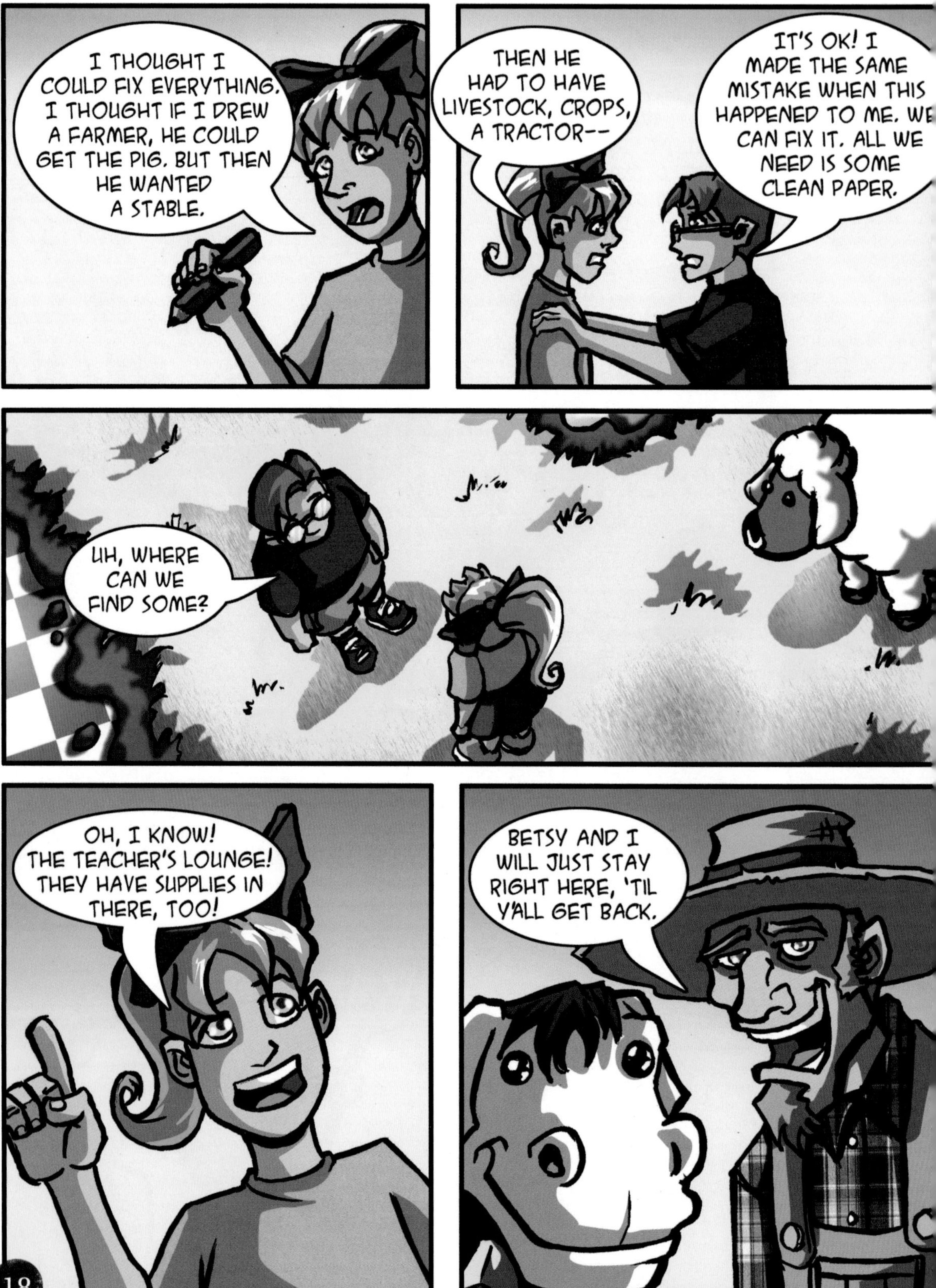
I THOUGHT I COULD FIX EVERYTHING. I THOUGHT IF I DREW A FARMER, HE COULD GET THE PIG. BUT THEN HE WANTED A STABLE.
THEN HE HAD TO HAVE LIVESTOCK, CROPS, A TRACTOR--
IT'S OK! I MADE THE SAME MISTAKE WHEN THIS HAPPENED TO ME. WE CAN FIX IT. ALL WE NEED IS SOME CLEAN PAPER.
UH, WHERE CAN WE FIND SOME?
OH, I KNOW! THE TEACHER'S LOUNGE! THEY HAVE SUPPLIES IN THERE, TOO!
BETSY AND I WILL JUST STAY RIGHT HERE, 'TIL Y'ALL GET BACK.

WAIT! WHAT HAPPENED TO MRS. ANDERSON?

NURSE'S STATION

YOUR CUTE LITTLE FLYING PIG HAPPENED! COME ON, THERE'S NO TIME TO STOP.

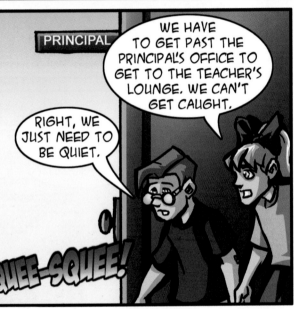

PRINCIPAL

WE HAVE TO GET PAST THE PRINCIPAL'S OFFICE TO GET TO THE TEACHER'S LOUNGE. WE CAN'T GET CAUGHT.

RIGHT, WE JUST NEED TO BE QUIET.

SQUEE-SQUEE!

NCIPAL

SQUEE-SQUEE!

I KNEW THIS PIZZA WAS TOO OLD TO EAT! I'M SEEING THINGS!

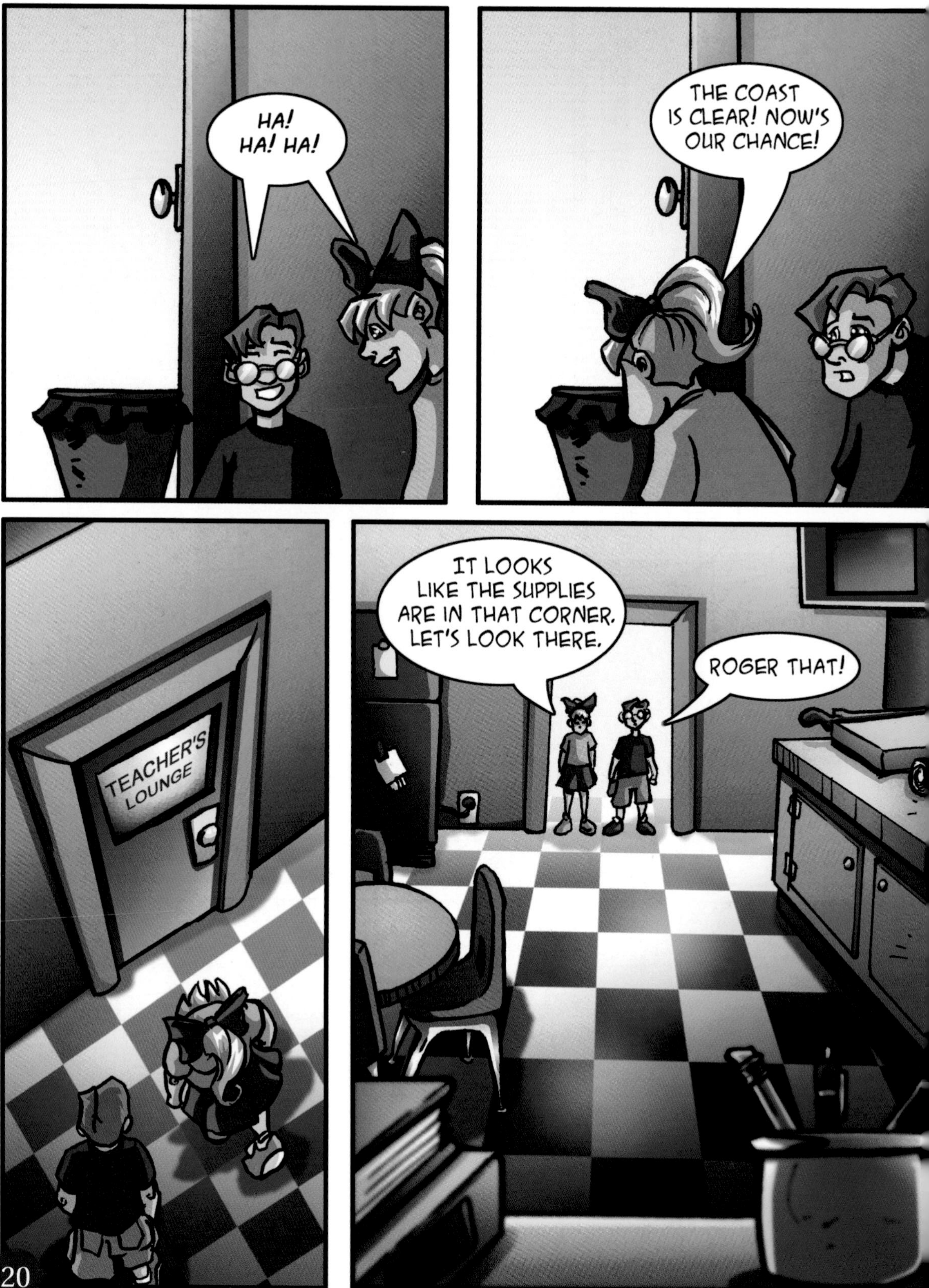
HA! HA! HA!
THE COAST IS CLEAR! NOW'S OUR CHANCE!
TEACHER'S LOUNGE
IT LOOKS LIKE THE SUPPLIES ARE IN THAT CORNER. LET'S LOOK THERE.
ROGER THAT!

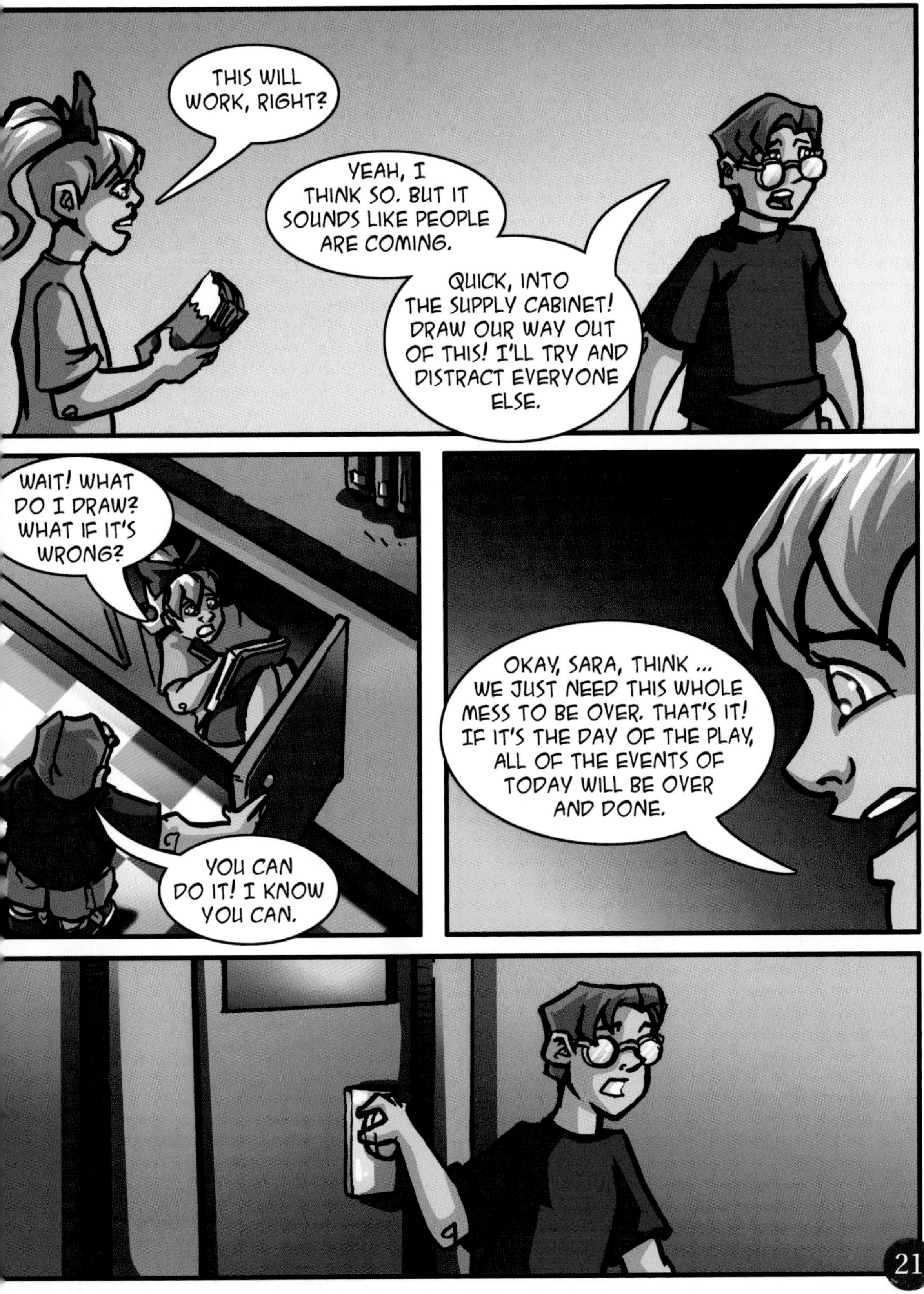
THIS WILL WORK, RIGHT?
YEAH, I THINK SO. BUT IT SOUNDS LIKE PEOPLE ARE COMING.
QUICK, INTO THE SUPPLY CABINET! DRAW OUR WAY OUT OF THIS! I'LL TRY AND DISTRACT EVERYONE ELSE.
WAIT! WHAT DO I DRAW? WHAT IF IT'S WRONG?
YOU CAN DO IT! I KNOW YOU CAN.
OKAY, SARA, THINK ... WE JUST NEED THIS WHOLE MESS TO BE OVER. THAT'S IT! IF IT'S THE DAY OF THE PLAY, ALL OF THE EVENTS OF TODAY WILL BE OVER AND DONE.

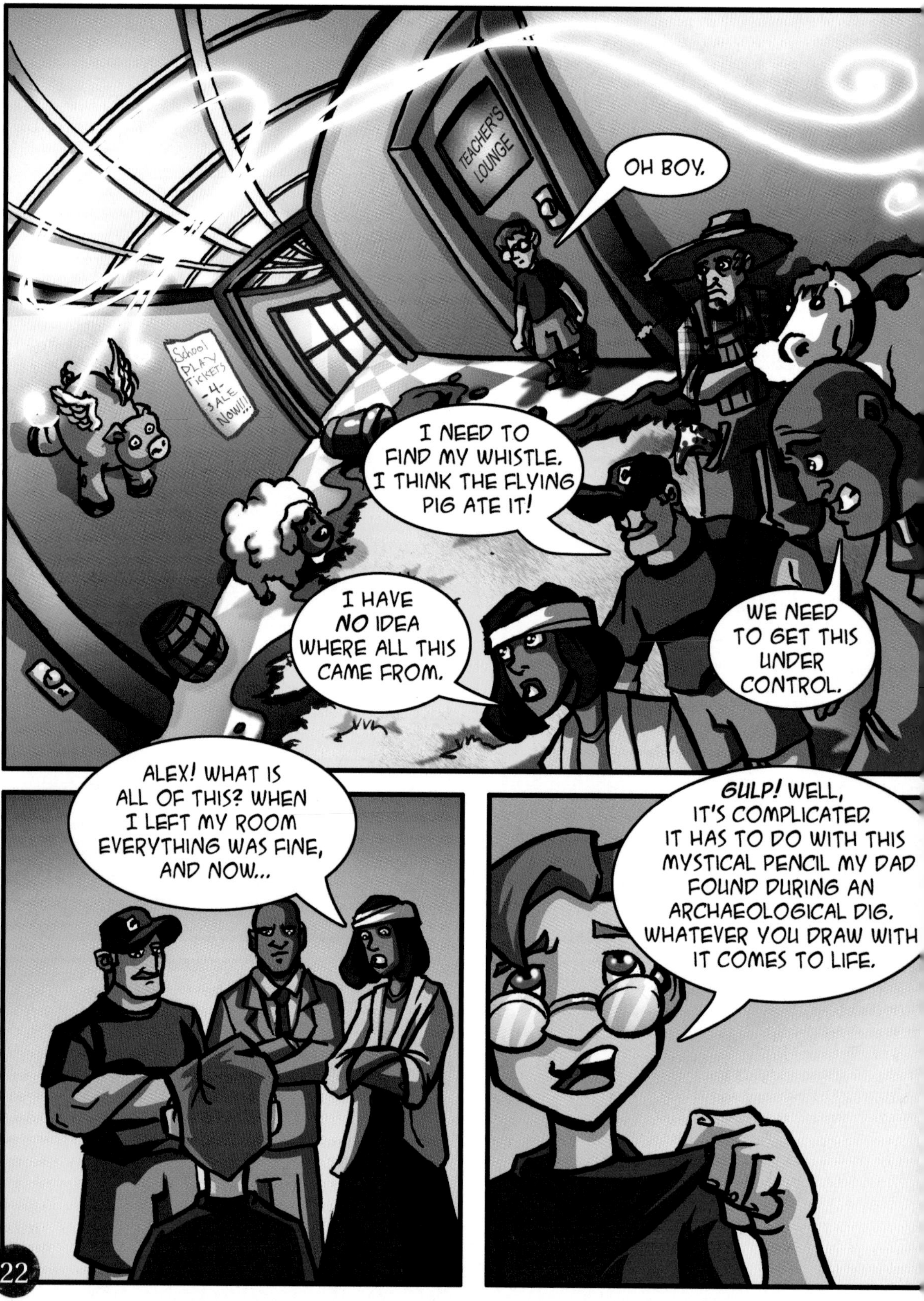
TEACHER'S LOUNGE
OH BOY.
School PLAY TICKETS -4- SALE NOW!!!
I NEED TO FIND MY WHISTLE. I THINK THE FLYING PIG ATE IT!
I HAVE NO IDEA WHERE ALL THIS CAME FROM.
WE NEED TO GET THIS UNDER CONTROL.
ALEX! WHAT IS ALL OF THIS? WHEN I LEFT MY ROOM EVERYTHING WAS FINE, AND NOW...
GULP! WELL, IT'S COMPLICATED. IT HAS TO DO WITH THIS MYSTICAL PENCIL MY DAD FOUND DURING AN ARCHAEOLOGICAL DIG. WHATEVER YOU DRAW WITH IT COMES TO LIFE.

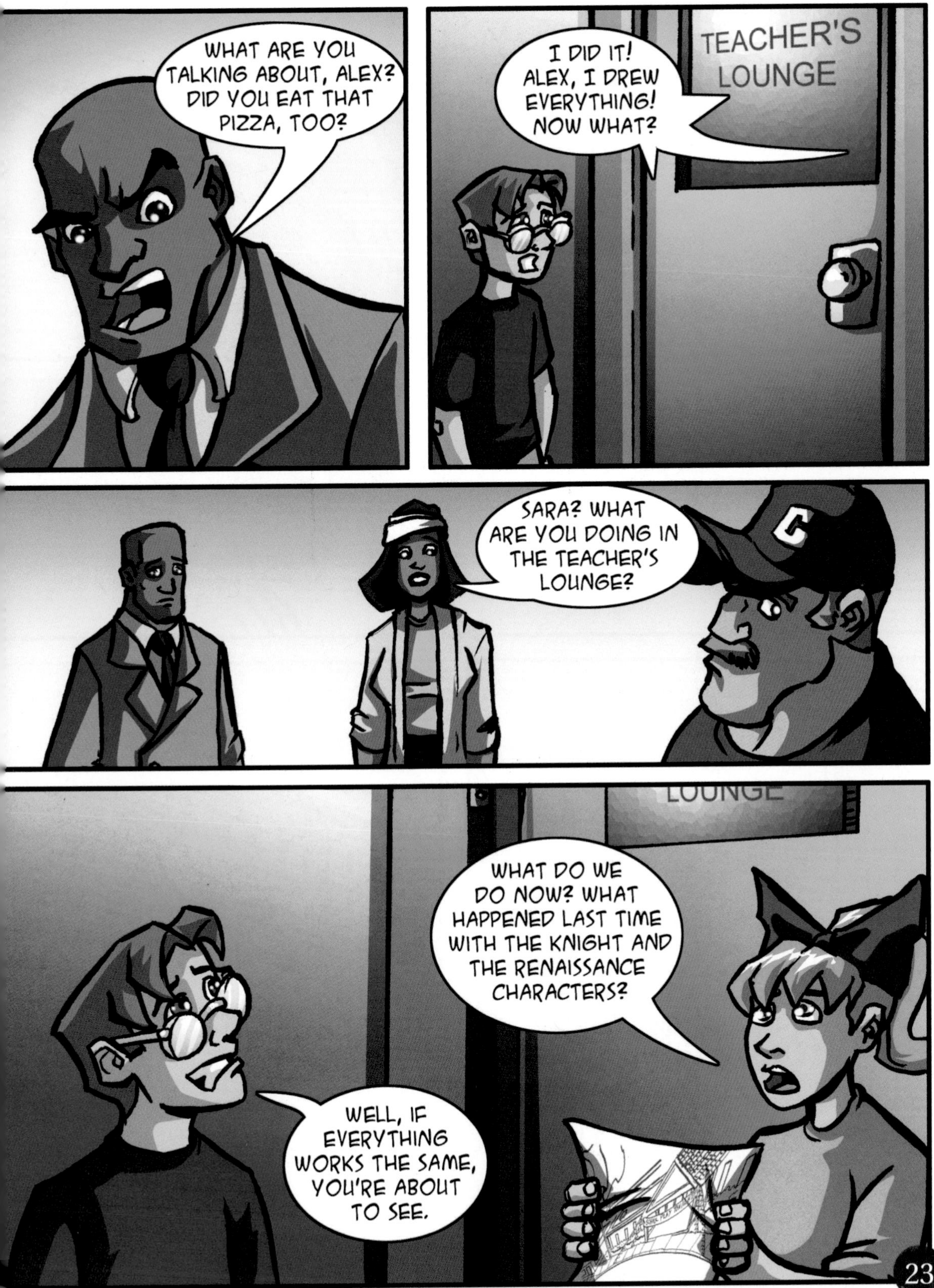
WHAT ARE YOU TALKING ABOUT, ALEX? DID YOU EAT THAT PIZZA, TOO?
TEACHER'S LOUNGE
I DID IT! ALEX, I DREW EVERYTHING! NOW WHAT?
SARA? WHAT ARE YOU DOING IN THE TEACHER'S LOUNGE?
LOUNGE
WHAT DO WE DO NOW? WHAT HAPPENED LAST TIME WITH THE KNIGHT AND THE RENAISSANCE CHARACTERS?
WELL, IF EVERYTHING WORKS THE SAME, YOU'RE ABOUT TO SEE.

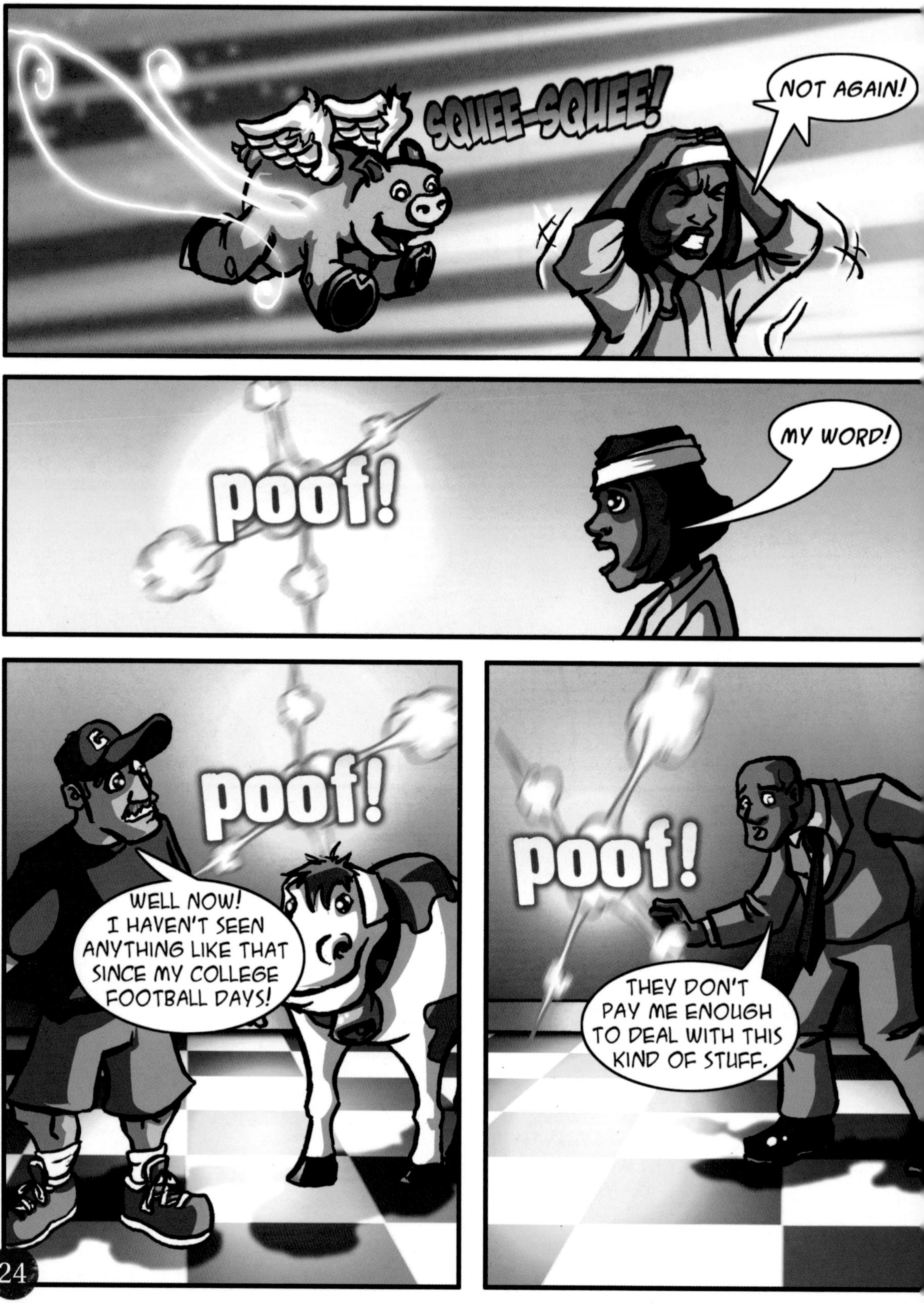
SQUEE-SQUEE!
NOT AGAIN!
poof!
MY WORD!
poof!
WELL NOW! I HAVEN'T SEEN ANYTHING LIKE THAT SINCE MY COLLEGE FOOTBALL DAYS!
poof!
THEY DON'T PAY ME ENOUGH TO DEAL WITH THIS KIND OF STUFF.

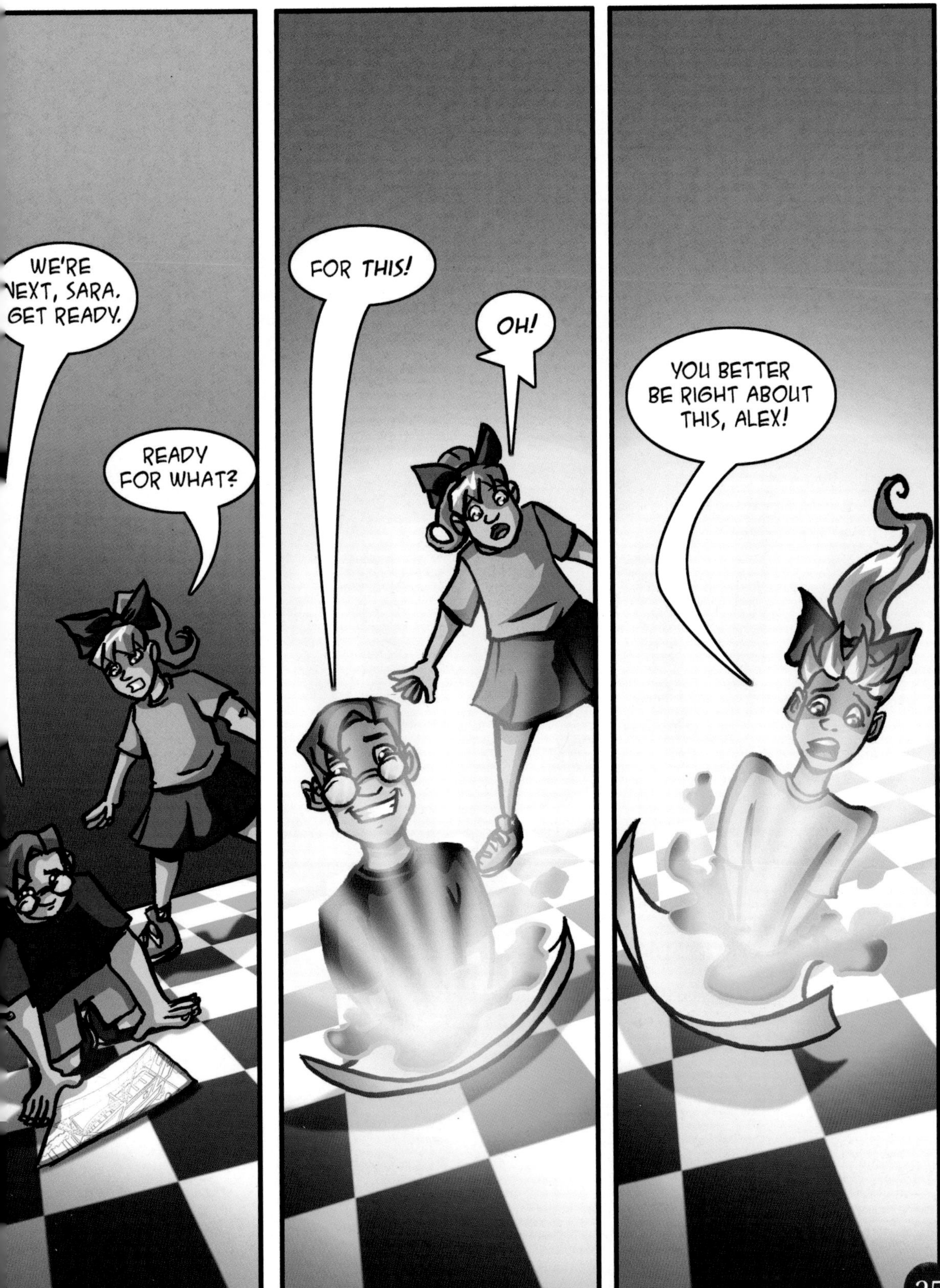
WE'RE NEXT, SARA. GET READY.
READY FOR WHAT?
FOR THIS!
OH!
YOU BETTER BE RIGHT ABOUT THIS, ALEX!

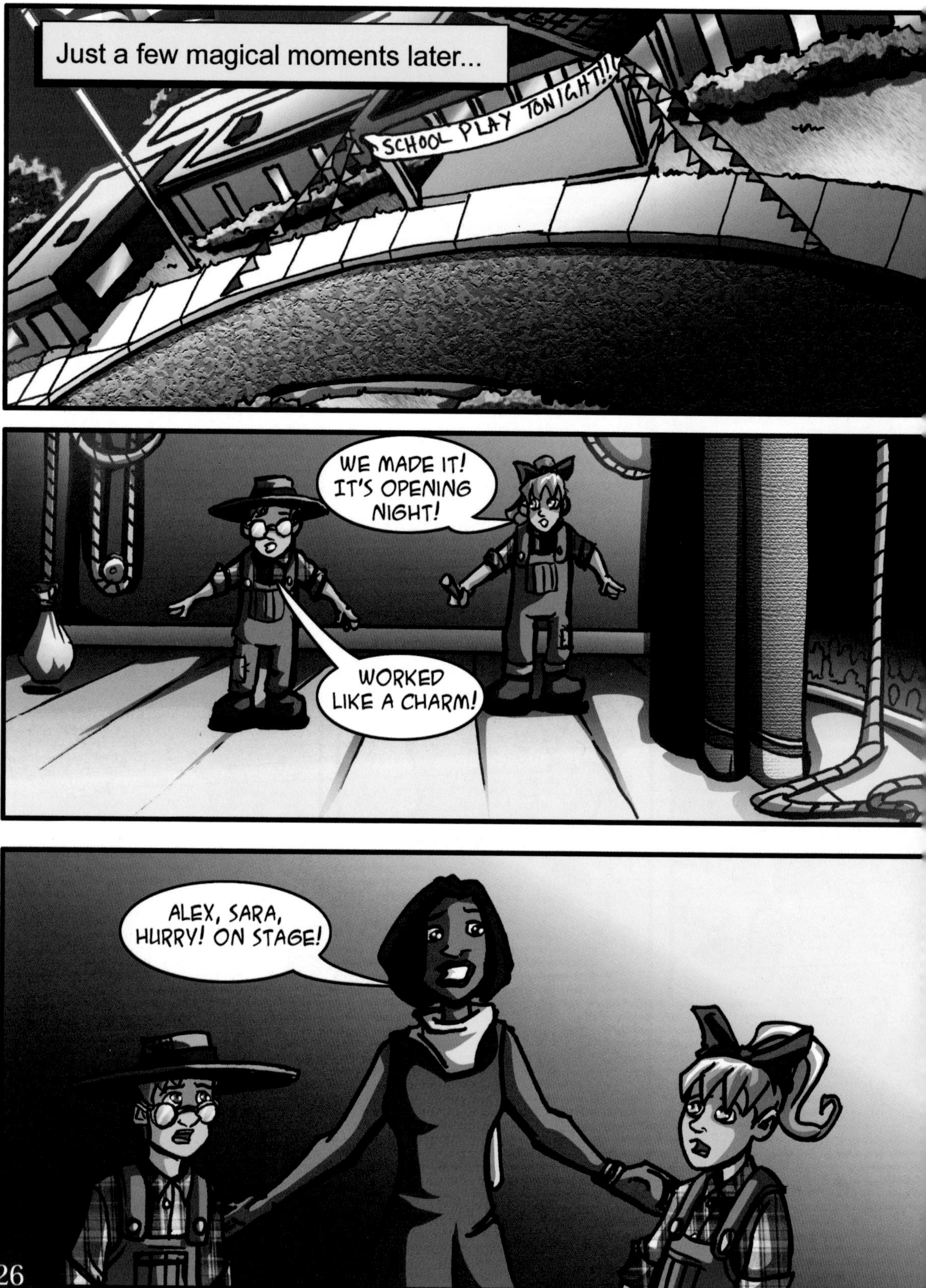
Just a few magical moments later...
SCHOOL PLAY TONIGHT!!
WE MADE IT! IT'S OPENING NIGHT!
WORKED LIKE A CHARM!
ALEX, SARA, HURRY! ON STAGE!

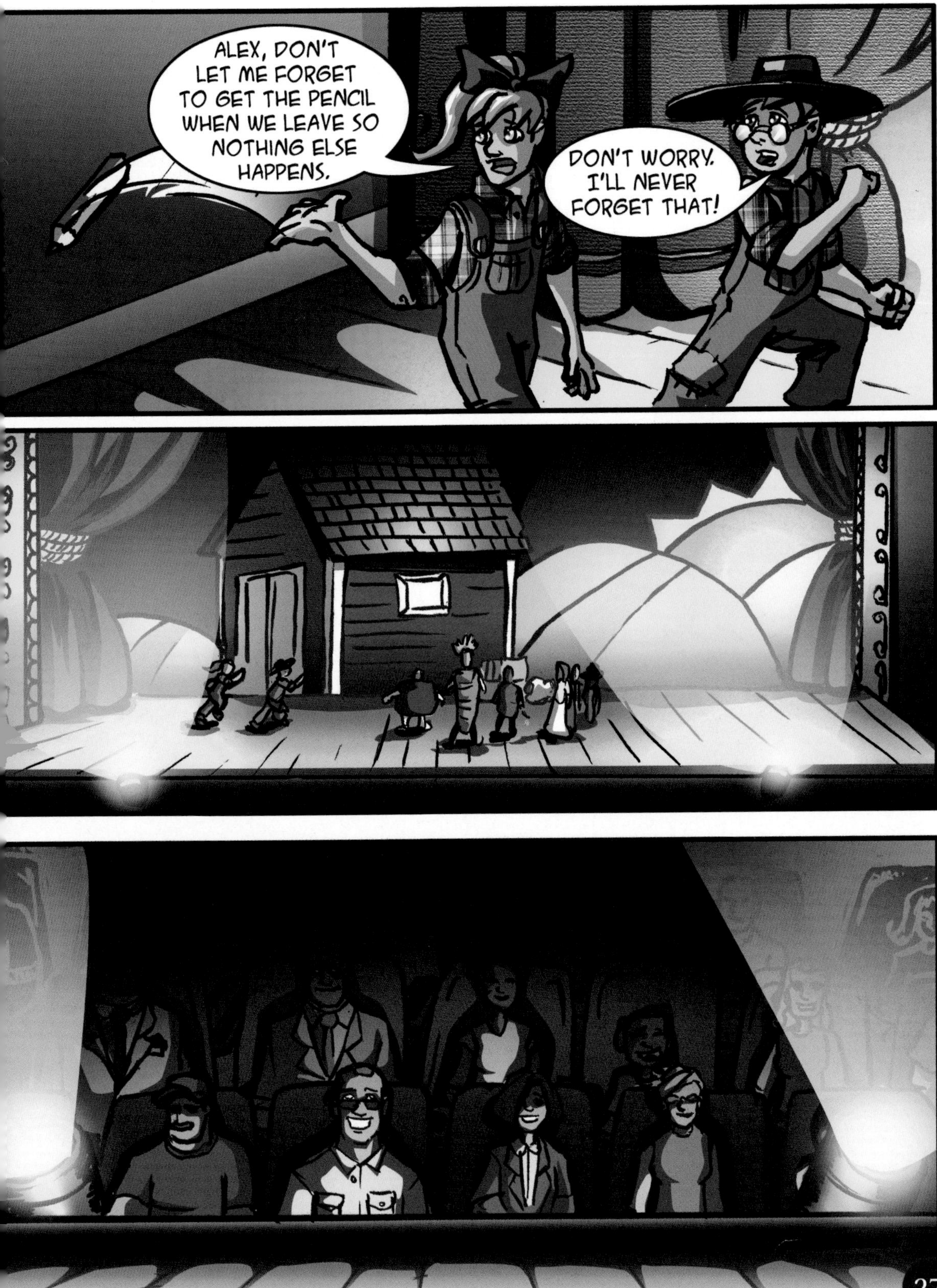
ALEX, DON'T LET ME FORGET TO GET THE PENCIL WHEN WE LEAVE SO NOTHING ELSE HAPPENS.
DON'T WORRY. I'LL NEVER FORGET THAT!

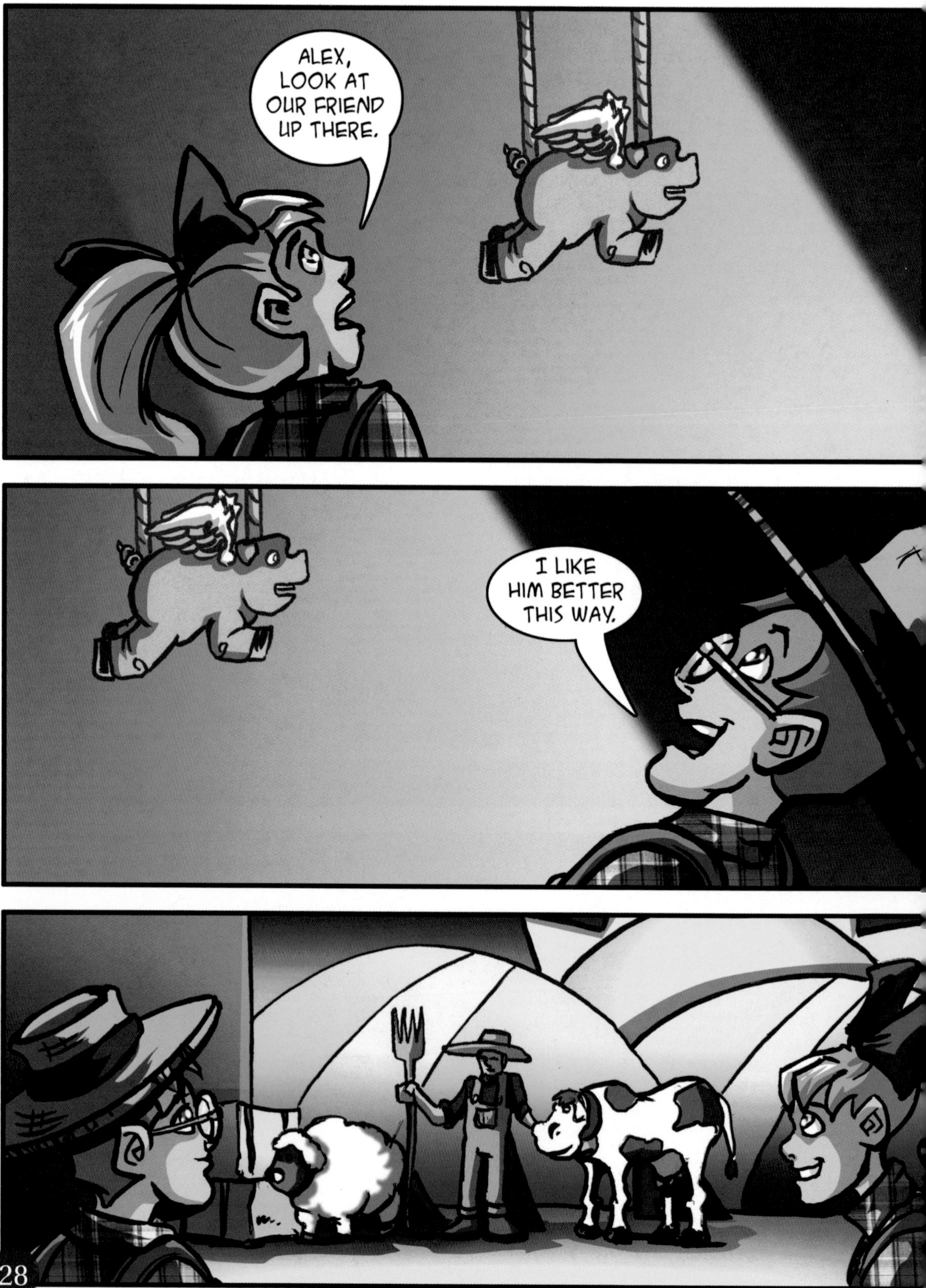
ALEX, LOOK AT OUR FRIEND UP THERE.
I LIKE HIM BETTER THIS WAY.

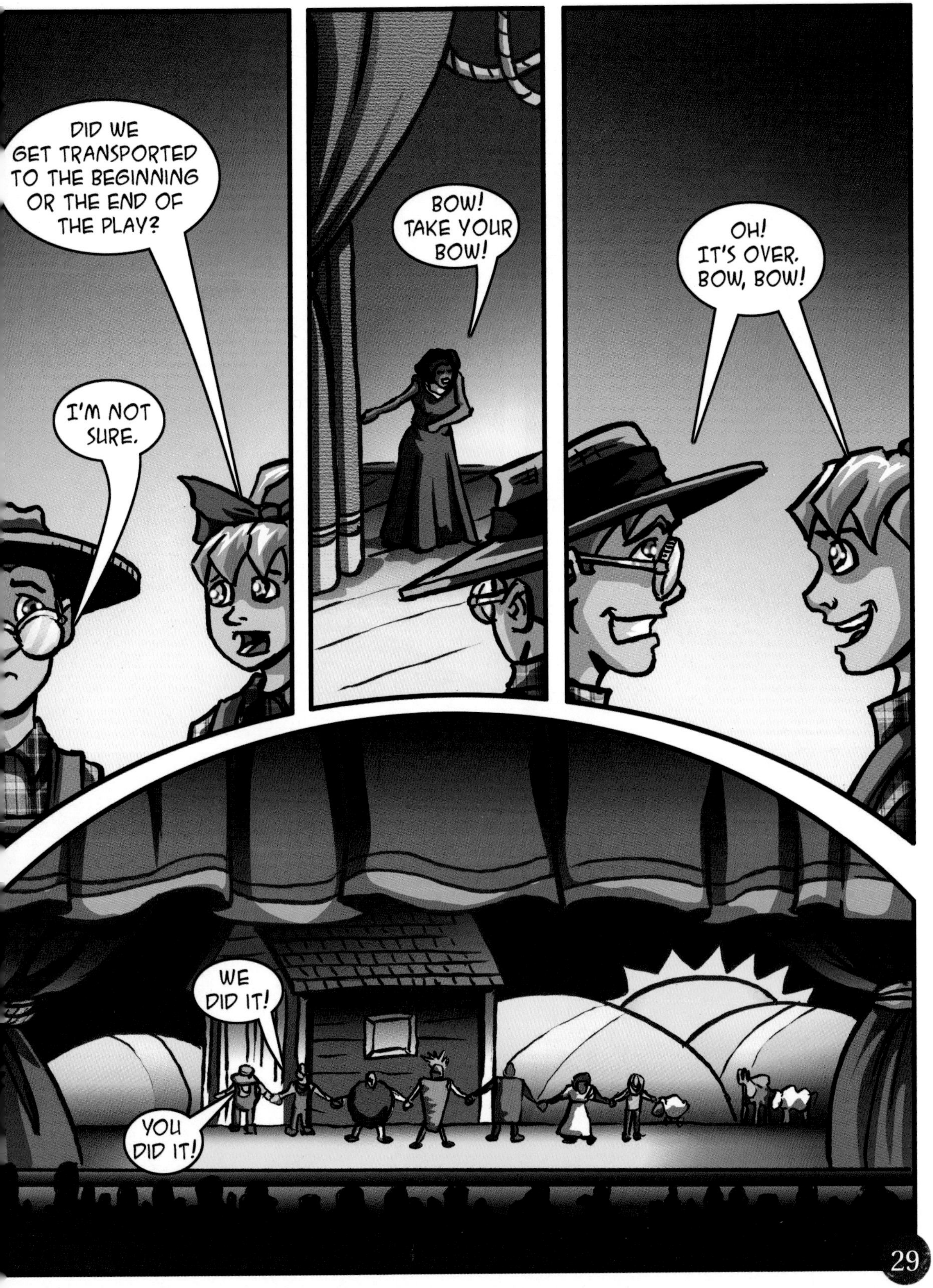
DID WE GET TRANSPORTED TO THE BEGINNING OR THE END OF THE PLAY?
I'M NOT SURE.
BOW! TAKE YOUR BOW!
OH! IT'S OVER. BOW, BOW!
WE DID IT!
YOU DID IT!

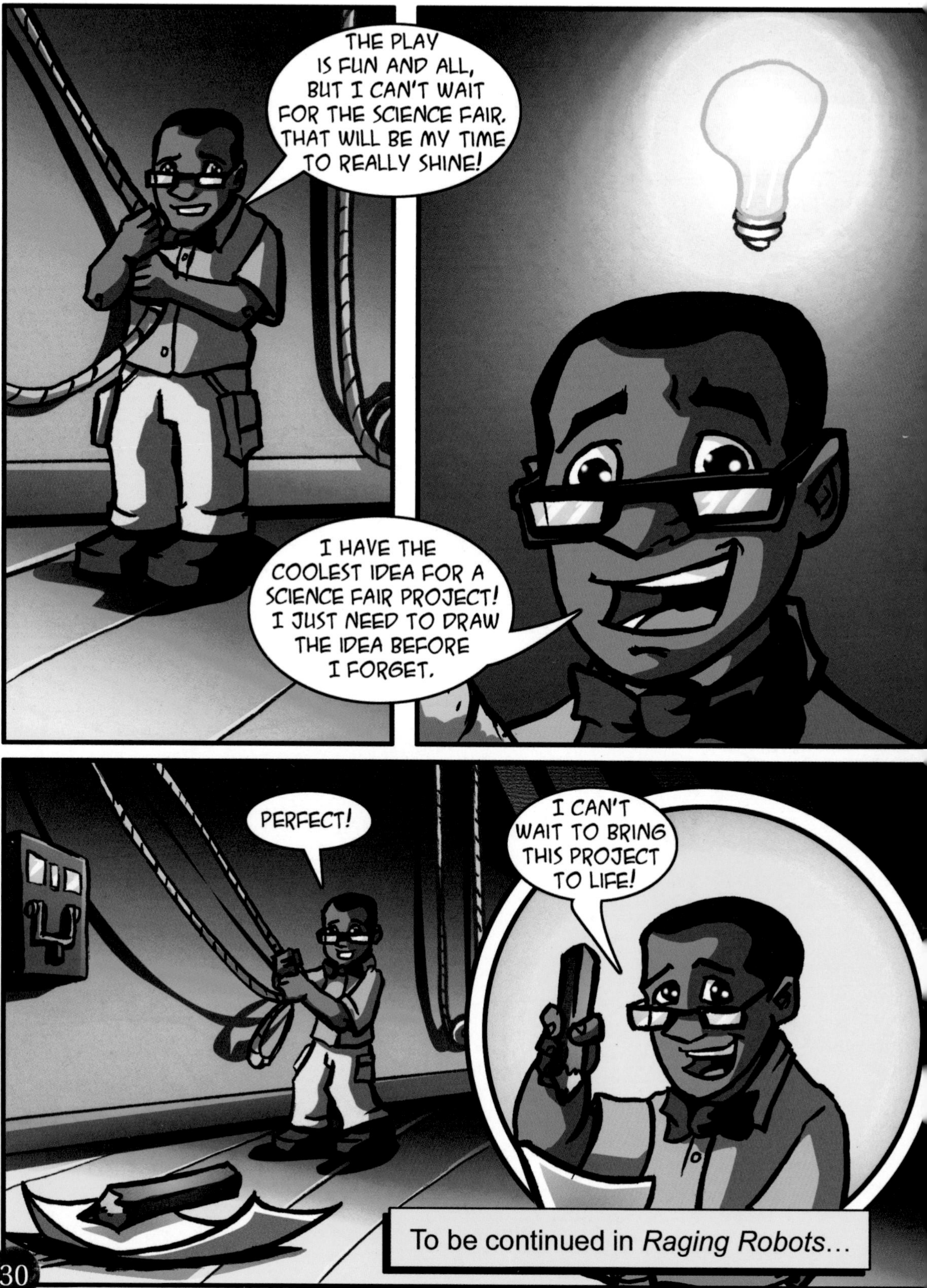
THE PLAY IS FUN AND ALL, BUT I CAN'T WAIT FOR THE SCIENCE FAIR. THAT WILL BE MY TIME TO REALLY SHINE!
I HAVE THE COOLEST IDEA FOR A SCIENCE FAIR PROJECT! I JUST NEED TO DRAW THE IDEA BEFORE I FORGET.
PERFECT!
I CAN'T WAIT TO BRING THIS PROJECT TO LIFE!
To be continued in *Raging Robots*…

How to Draw a Flying Pig

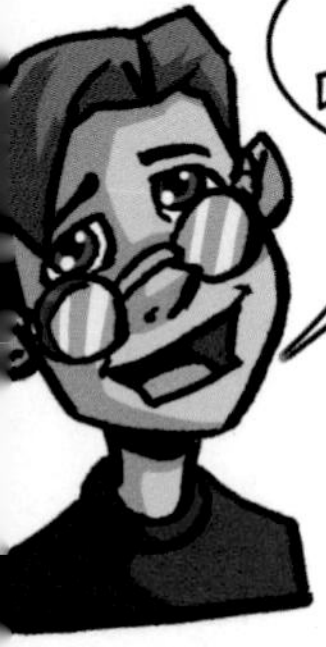
WE'RE GOING TO LEARN HOW TO DRAW A FLYING PIG!
THE SUPPLIES YOU NEED ARE A PENCIL, ERASER, AND SOME PAPER.

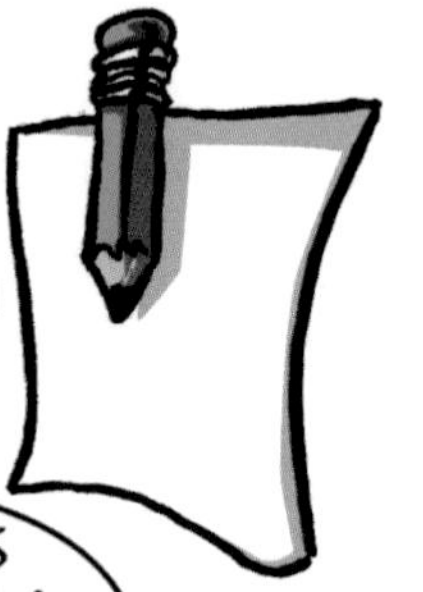

1 START BY USING BASIC SHAPES TO SKETCH THE SHAPE OF THE PIG. USE CIRCLES, OVALS, CYLINDERS, AND TRIANGLES.

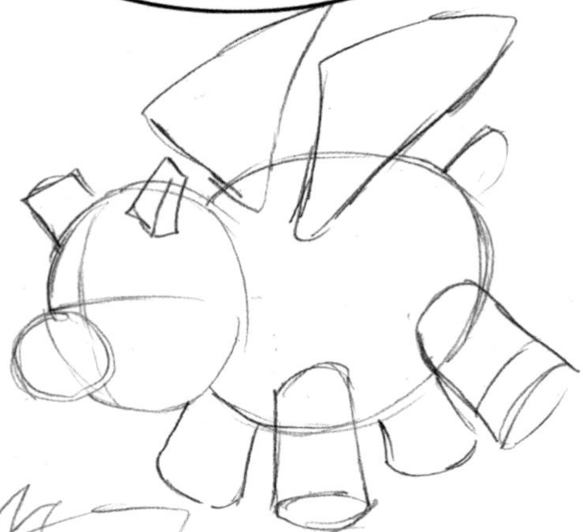

2 ERASE THE LINES YOU DON'T NEED, LIKE THE LINE BEHIND THE WING AND EARS. YOU CAN ALSO ADD SOME DETAILS LIKE THE SHAPE OF THE TAIL, WHERE THE EYES WILL GO, AND FEATHERS ON THE WINGS.

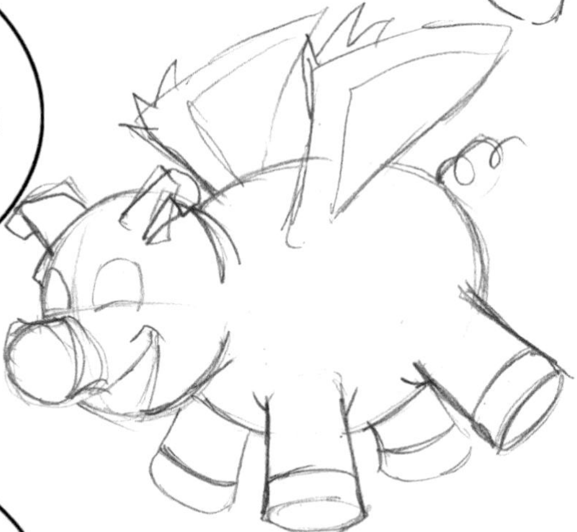

3 BE CREATIVE AND MAKE THE PIG COME TO LIFE. ADD DETAILS TO THE NOSE, EYES, MOUTH, AND WINGS. ADD SOME MOTION LINES TO MAKE IT LOOK LIKE THE PIG IS REALLY FLYING!

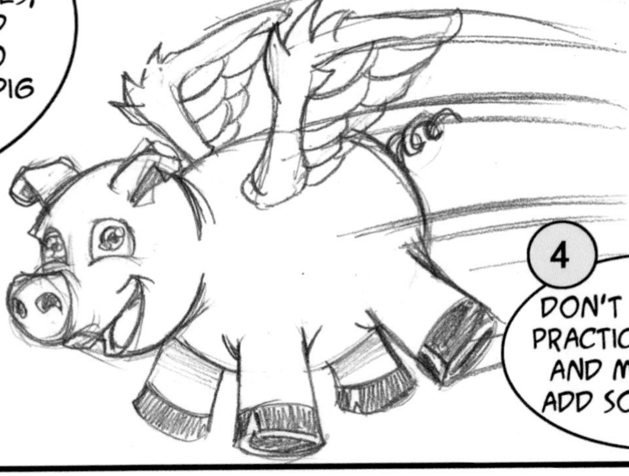

4 DON'T FORGET TO PRACTICE. HAVE FUN AND MAYBE EVEN ADD SOME COLOR!

About the Author

Dustin Evans was born and raised in Oklahoma. In 2005, Dustin graduated from Oklahoma State University with a BFA in Graphic Design & Illustration. He has since gone on to work with such companies as Disney, IDW Publishing, Magic Wagon, and more. His work can be seen in comic books and children's books and on apparel and TV. He enjoys spending time with his family and pets, reading, drawing, and going to museums and movies.

Dustin begins each page with simple pencil and paper. Working from the script, he creates a rough layout for each page. Once the layouts are ready, he then scans the images into the computer to make them larger. The next step is to print out the larger layout, transfer it to the final page using a light box, and then ink the final image. Dustin then goes back to the computer to scan the final, inked image. Now it's time to add digital color, special effects, and lettering using computer programs. Finally, the image is complete and ready for print after some fine-tuning with any needed edits.

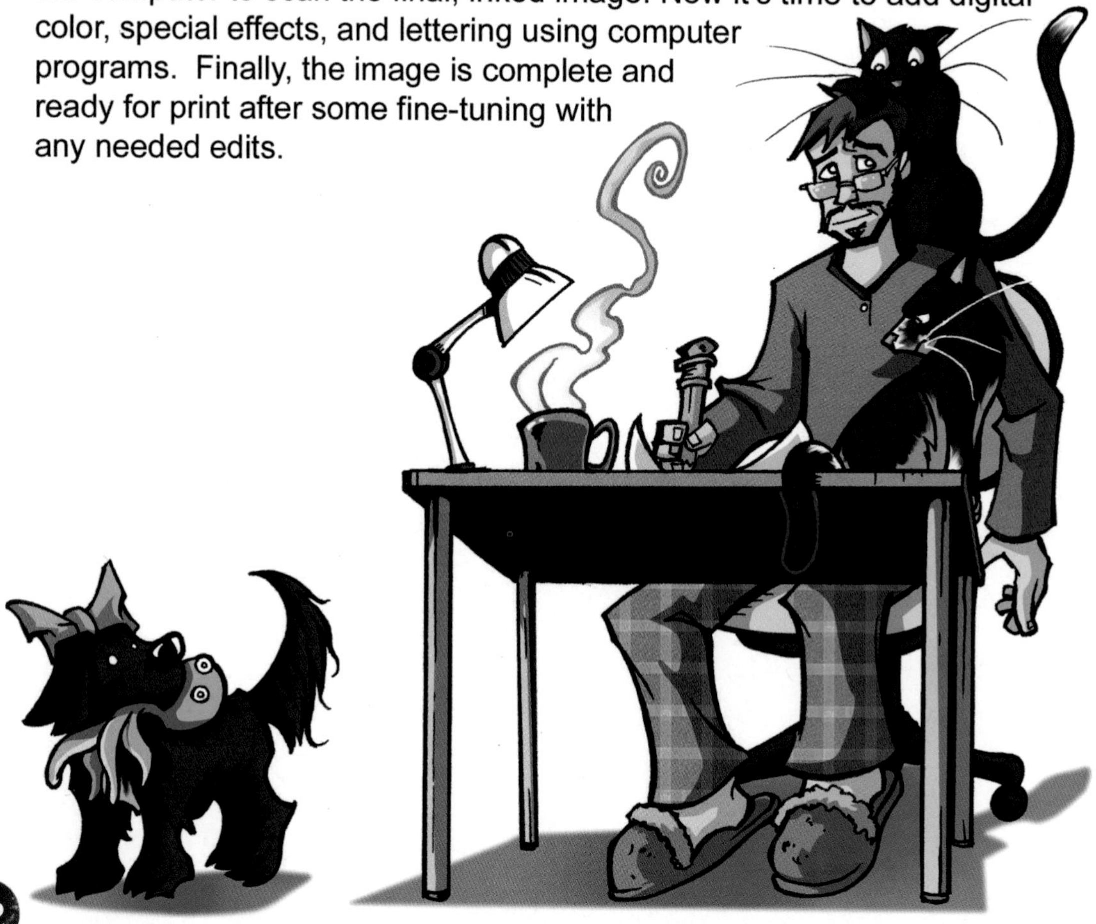